NORTHERN CREATURES

"I am Victorsson, son of Victor—son of the abandoning father who called himself Frankenstein. I am an unsettled soul.

"The elves call me Frank..."

— MONSTER BORN

MONSTER BORN

NORTHERN CREATURES BOOK ONE

KRIS AUSTEN RADCLIFFE

THE WORLDS OF

KRIS AUSTEN RADCLIFFE

Smart Urban Fantasy:

Northern Creatures

Monster Born

Vampire Cursed

Elf Raised

Wolf Hunted

Fae Touched (*coming soon*)

*Genre-bending Science Fiction about
love, family, and dragons:*

WORLD ON FIRE

Series one

Fate Fire Shifter Dragon

Games of Fate

Flux of Skin

Fifth of Blood

Bonds Broken & Silent

All But Human

Men and Beasts

The Burning World

Dragon's Fate and Other Stories

MONSTER BORN

NORTHERN CREATURES
Book One

By
Kris Austen Radcliffe

Six Talon Sign Fantasy & Futuristic Romance
Minneapolis

www.krisaustenradcliffe.com

Published by
Six Talon Sign Fantasy & Futuristic Romance

Edited by Annetta Ribken
Copyedited by Juli Lilly
"Northern Creatures" artwork created by Christina Rausch
Cover to be designed by Covers by Christian
Plus a special thanks to my Proofing Crew.

For requests, please e-mail: publisher@sixtalonsign.com.

First print edition, August 2017
Version: 10.14.2019

ISBN: 978-1-939730-46-6

MONSTER BORN

CHAPTER 1

I am an unsettled soul. I lumber through the accumulation of my two-hundred-plus years and yet somehow, under my thick fingers, the delicate stones of a precious grave marker did not wobble.

Lizzy's cairn held its shape.

The stones, each individually lifted from the pebbled lakeshore behind me, continued their duty. Each locked to the ones above and below, and each held steadfast.

Two centuries ago, I set the first stone, a flat, cracked wedge of granite I'd found up the hill. Cold soil had folded around my equally cold hands as I'd dug it out. Dark soil full of bits of life—beetles and ants and the parts of leaves rendered into grains—squished between my fingers. I carried the stone to the cairn's site and pressed it into the moss under what had been, at the time, an oak sapling. Another two rocks—one a purplish-red, semi-smooth lake stone, and the other a gray, boxy, small boulder—set the cairn's foundation.

To this day, I still tended the grave marker. I still visited.

"Lizzy," I whispered. She had run the Arctic with me. She had kept me alive. If it hadn't been for her and the other hounds of my sled team, I would have sunk below the ice long before we found new land.

My trek had started with one blazing moment of rage. One

singular need to make my father pay for his trespasses against not only me, but life itself.

He escaped. I rode my fury into the midnight sun, a modern Prometheus on the back of a sled pulled by hounds with souls stronger than my own.

I hunted seal. The dogs ran until only Lizzy remained. And one day, she and I wandered into magic.

She died shortly after the elves found us. They thought me a *jotunn* —a giant. Many of them still do. I no longer argue.

The werewolves understood Lizzy's soul. They helped me choose the sapling that marked her grave. The two *loup-garou* pack founders, Gerard and Remy Geroux, went so far as to declare the oak sacred to their kind. And slowly, over the years and decades, I slotted into Lizzy's cairn a new quartz chip here, an open agate geode there. I fitted the smooth and the pockmarked. With the wolves' help, I built for Lizzy a marker worthy of her bright light.

The sapling became one of the many grand oaks circling my lake. Above my head, a squirrel ran the branches chattering like Ratatoskr filling the eagle Vedrfolnir's head with gossip. The lake lapped its shore. The sun warmed my skin and I wondered about my unsettled soul. I wondered how it was that a hound always knew with certainty the reality of her world.

I set a new stone, one with a rounded edge perfect for the tree-side of the cairn, and stepped back.

I am large by both mundane human and elf standards. I duck and twist my shoulders when crossing most thresholds, and stand a good nine inches taller than Arne Odinsson, the elf who oversees this land. My eyes, though dark, shimmer with a deep red fire. I wear my black hair in the Old Norse style the elves prefer—naked above my ears and twisted into a knot at the back of my head. But unlike the natural pattern of the elves, I must shave my scalp where my scars do not already inhibit my hair's growth.

The scars have faded over my two centuries, and the slow rebuilding of my epidermis has replaced my original sallowness with a warm, if ashen, demi-health. I was built from parts of others, after all, and modeled out of clay polluted with death. My health is not my own.

I am the abandoned son of a mad scientist. I am a man who walked the Arctic into a new continent, and a monster adopted by Nordic New World elves. I am friend to werewolves, witches, and vampires.

I am Victorsson, son of Victor—son of the abandoning father who called himself Frankenstein. I am an unsettled soul.

The elves call me Frank.

CHAPTER 2

I liked my home. I'd added and subtracted over the years, including modernizing with argon-filled, insulating windows, the latest in solar and battery technology, and new plumbing with a reverse-osmosis water filtration system. The cabin wasn't too big or too small, and even though it was now two centuries old, it continued to work well for me.

My lake spanned several hectares and curved around a peninsula. I built my cabin shortly after Arne found me, and the tree that gave its life to become the log walls of my home might very well have been the father of the grand oak that now shaded Lizzy's cairn.

The lake and the land around it were part of the Red River Colony when I arrived. The people here were Scots, French, and English, except for the elves. They were of the magical Scandinavian cultures, Norwegians mostly, and had crossed the Atlantic with their mundane human explorers a good seven centuries before other Europeans entered the area. Unlike their Norse, the elves never abandoned their toehold on the new continent, and instead used their magic to sail the waterways inland, to the Great Lakes and to the forests surrounding the headwaters of the Mississippi River.

The elves kept to themselves, and even though they traded with the local tribes, they bothered no one, nor did they share their magic, demand tributes, or steal anyone's children.

They built houses of wood and they fished the streams. They listened to the wind and they walked with the natural world of North America. They lived in their village and they glamoured only to trade.

Now they controlled not only the town of Alfheim, Minnesota, but also the county territory around it, including my lake.

Plots were mapped, and utilities routed. Lake homes designed. "Tourism brings in money," Arne liked to say.

Tourists, who came into town looking for rental cabins or property to buy. Mundane, normal people wanting a weekend up north, near the Boundary Waters, where they might—just *might*—see a timber wolf.

Or a werewolf, if they weren't careful during the full moon. Or, if they needed to check a book out of our library, or place a bet with a bookie, one of our two vampires.

Or an elf with a bow or staff.

Or me, the abominable son of a long-dead mad man, the local "giant" named Frank Victorsson.

Not that the mundanes noticed. Or at least I hoped they didn't notice. The new construction on the opposite side of my lake had me wondering.

Three connected sections. One building. Lots of reflective glass. Some rich person from Minneapolis wanted a getaway lake home and had decided that he preferred Alfheim's economy and tourist amenities over the other local small cities. Bemidji had its charms, as did Ely, but the elves loved artists—glass blowers, painters, sculptors—which people from The Cities seemed to enjoy.

So other than my current houseguests, I was about to have neighbors for the first time in my two centuries living in Alfheim, Minnesota. Wealthy neighbors who were likely to spend a lot of money on local color.

The sun hit one of the pointy window protrusions. I shifted on my mat where I sat on my deck, and squinted. So much for my morning lakeside meditation.

I learned long ago to be mindful of my inner workings. Bad outcomes happened when I lumbered about raging against a bitter universe.

I was no longer that man. Two hundred years of watching humanity pass by had taught me that no matter the injustice or the slight suffered, it too shall pass. Besides, a giant raging maniac did not make a good host, and when one hosts elves, one needed to be on point.

So I breathed in the late summer lake air. I cleared my mind of my body's need to attend to the parts of the world that did not need attending. Waves lapped. Trees rustled. The sun beat down on my face and my dog chased salamanders. At least for one morning, all was right.

Until the saws and the pounding started.

I wrapped my cold fingers around my tea. Meditating in the sun helped warm my cold flesh; otherwise, sitting on a pillow and thinking about nothing cooled down my body, which only serves to highlight my more corpse-like traits.

Women do not enjoy waking up next to a man who needed to sunbathe on a rock like a damned lizard in order to feel touchable. Winter, summer, northern forests or tropical climates, it doesn't matter. My mad father built me to sleep like the dead. At least my dogs never minded.

With my new neighbors, it seemed as if I would no longer have the option of peacefully sunning my tired bones. I sipped my tea, then pulled my t-shirt over my head.

Hammering echoed across my lake. The coming autumn-crisped the air and the changing leaves were a week or so from fiery reds and golds. Sounds travel better in cold air, and soon I would be listening to laughter and loud parties.

Samhain was a month away but had begun flavoring the universe. Festivals and parties bounced through town and the lakes like dancing clowns. Apples this week. Next week, water fowl. The tourists loved it and the parties all led up to an elven week of hidden Samhain mystery which I did my best to ignore.

I hauled my bulk to its full, noticeable-across-the-lake height. My neighbors were not shaping up into anything I would label as "tolerable."

A boom ricocheted over the lake. Swearing followed. A saw started up.

No, my new neighbors were not anything close to tolerable.

Inside, my refrigerator door slammed against the cabinets. The youngest of my two houseguests must be packing her school lunch.

I sipped my tea. My dog-emperor, Marcus Aurelius, barked and ran into the house, obviously questing for one last hug and pat from my adoptive niece.

Marcus Aurelius was a large, staunch dog, sized correctly for me, with golden, curly fur and a bright hound mind. I had no idea what his breed might be; I'd rescued him from the side of the road in the middle of a particularly brisk winter and he'd been my companion ever since.

I followed him toward the wide French doors that separate the deck area of my home from the kitchen.

Maura Dagsdottir walked in from the hallway at the same time I closed the doors. She glamoured down her radiance—and her ears— for the real world. To the mundane humans of Alfheim, she looked like many women of Scandinavian heritage—tall, nicely curved, gray-eyed, with angular features and a big brown ponytail. Today she wore a t-shirt and jeans much like my own, as did Akeyla.

This morning, Maura's magic flickered.

I see magic. It manifests as auras and shimmers in my visual perception. None of the elves quite understand when I describe for them my sensations. Neither do the wolves. Arne frowns and says my "seeing" magic is akin to him tasting a color, or hearing a number.

It is what it is, and the elves occasionally find my gift useful.

"You okay?" I made a small gesture to indicate the sparking in her natural magic aura.

Maura stopped in the hallway's threshold. Her eyes narrowed. I may be her adoptive brother, but I was not to speak of such things in front of Akeyla.

Maura threw me a small, consolatory smile, then dropped her glamour as she walked into the room. Her black hair glistened with the blues and shimmering purples of winter, and the protection enchantments tattooed around her scalp picked up those icy colors. She was, in many ways, the exact opposite of her ex. Maura was slow and steady, like an ice floe; and also like a floe, when she cracked, all hell broke loose.

"I'm good," Maura said.

As good as she was going to admit, more like it. Sometimes I wished she would talk to me about the wounds in her magic. I'd offered help several times. Maura was as stubborn as every other elf in Alfheim, and wasn't likely to seek support unless she was literally bleeding out.

But at least she had decided to stay with "Uncle Frank" until she and Akeyla could find a suitable place of their own. With elves, a "suitable" place had to be magically suitable as well as mundanely accessible, and Maura was particularly picky. Akeyla, being half fire spirit, had a uniqueness to her that required extra magical work.

I didn't pretend to understand. I could, though, offer a safe place to live until all was magically correct.

I walked over and gave Maura a quick side-on shoulder hug. She looked up at my face and some of the morning pain seemed to fade.

Akeyla slammed the refrigerator door hard enough that the entire kitchen rattled.

I walked back toward the center island and set my mug on the granite counter. "Careful with that, pumpkin," I said.

A wave of Akeyla's fire elf warmth spread through the kitchen like a magical tsunami, all flickering and golden and flowing more like water than heat. She grinned and set her lunch next to my mug.

"You warm, Uncle Frank?" she asked.

"I am." I squatted and held out my arms for a hug.

The little elf I called niece burst forward all full of smiles and wild child energy, her own arms spread wide and her wavy black hair bundled into a poof on the back of her head.

"Yah!" she squealed, and jumped into my embrace.

I swung her up to my hip. Like her mother, Akeyla had the tall, pointed ears of an elf. She looked like Maura as well, with an oval face and a strong, curved set to her lips. But she also looked like her fire spirit father.

Which meant darker, warmer skin than the Nordic elves. She lacked the bald band around her scalp as well, which decreased her canvas area for enchantment and protection tattoos. And her eyes looked more like my own dark mahogany, reddish irises than her mother's pale gray.

Akeyla's glamour hid her ears from the mundanes, but not her elven and spirit features. Such intricate, delicate glamours were the domain of the adult elves like Maura, and not even all of them could handle appearing fully "normal."

"Looks like it's going to be a nice day," Maura said as she reached up to rub a smudge off Akeyla's cheek.

"Mom!" My little niece pulled away and buried her face in my shoulder.

Maura grinned. "You're her favorite uncle, ya know."

No, I didn't mind one bit having house guests.

Maura tapped the counter. "We'll pick up macadamia nuts on the way home."

"Oh!" I exaggerated for Akeyla. "Are we making dessert tonight?"

You learn a lot about the world when you live with elves. Useful knowledge drips off them like honeydew—sweet, addictive, and sticky as hell. Once you've learned a way from an elf, there's no turning back.

Especially when it came to making brownies. Not the "squat little hobgoblin" kind. The close-to-godliness, fudge kind.

"Yep!" Akeyla kissed my cheek.

I knew they'd be moving out soon, but I had to admit I liked having them here.

9

"So we *have* to use Dutch process cocoa? That's the rule?" I asked.

My young supervisor scrunched up her eight-year-old face as I set her down next to the kitchen counter.

Her crunched-up lips released into a big grin and her magic danced around her little body. She wisped her delicate hand through the air. "*Duh*, Uncle Frank." She rolled her eyes. "Otherwise the magic won't work."

With elves, rules equal magic, and magic equals sweet, addictive, sticky brownies.

"Oh," I said, and nodded once as if I'd finally learned the true meaning of life.

Akeyla patted my arm. "That's okay. Mommy says you're super smart." She said it in a way that made me think the jury was still out on my smartness.

By the refrigerator, Maura covered a snort by pretending to cough.

I leaned down as if to share with Akeyla a secret of great importance. "It's not the smarts that make me super," I said. "It's little elf hugs!"

I scooped her up off her stool and twirled her high up over my head. She screeched as only an eight-year-old can—an unearthly loud, high-pitched, kid-giggle—and stuck her arms out at her sides.

"I'm flying!" She screeched again.

At my almost seven foot height and with a reach and speed that were significantly more "super" than my smarts, I pretty much did have her flying.

Her elemental fire magic licked at the ceiling as dancing, barely visible, red and blue pseudo-flames. They carried heat, but not the chaotic release of energy that came with a blaze. The heat of a fire elf touched souls.

Akeyla Maurasdottir would one day be an elf worthy of both adoration and terror.

Maura's cell phone rang. "Hello?" she said.

I twirled Akeyla again, then used her to do a couple one-armed press-ups.

That got the giggles going.

Maura frowned and looked up at the ceiling. "No, no, Sam." She sighed. "I *do* trust your judgement to pick the best place, but I need to check them."

Samantha Nelson, the mundane owner of Alfheim's Nelson Florals. A call from Sam meant that Akeyla's father had sent yet another bouquet. He was, as Maura's mother said, "creepily persistent."

Maura had left Alfheim for Hawaii about a decade ago, but came home with Akeyla two months ago. Her ex did a number on her—the bruising of her magic. The sparking where there should have been silk-like sheets.

This morning's flickering.

Sam didn't understand why Maura or Dag needed to check the card and the flowers before she sent the arrangements on to the hospital or the schools. She wasn't one of the handful of mundanes in town who knew about magic.

But the card, message, and flowers needed to be checked. Sometimes magic could be "creepily persistent" even if the spell used Sam's own flowers.

I watched the lovely child giggling and flying over my head. "I'm going to have to put you down, pumpkin," I said. The continued bad behavior of Maura's ex took precedent.

Akeyla scowled and purposefully arched her back like an ice skater in the middle of a lift. I flipped her onto my shoulders. "Watch your head." I bounced her around the kitchen.

"Looks like we're leaving for school early today." Maura held up her phone. "I need to check on this."

I nodded and set Akeyla down. "Sure thing."

"Mom!" Akeyla pouted and stomped her foot. "We don't need to leave for school for another *fifteen minutes.*"

Maura squatted down to her daughter's level. "I know, honey. But we need to go so I can check in with Sam." She looked up at me.

I squatted down, too. "Tell you what. We'll go fishing tomorrow."

Akeyla bounced. "Can we take Marcus Aurelius?"

My dog nuzzled her hand.

"Of course we can," I said.

She bounced on her toes. "All right!" She grabbed her lunch off the counter. "Bye, Uncle Frank!"

And after one final hug, I sent my elven sister and niece off to town.

CHAPTER 3

I watched Maura's sedan pull away as she and Akeyla made their way down my gravel driveway. Maura would drop Akeyla at school, then make her way to Nelson's Floral. I'd spend my day alone with my noisy neighbors.

Marcus Aurelius padded over and sat his big hound backside next to my foot. The werewolves liked Marcus Aurelius, and Gerard and Remy often asked to borrow him to comfort the occasional, also-rescued, new pack member. Times like this, I understood why.

My dear dog wagged his tail.

"You want to go for a ride, don't you?" I looked back at the house. I was low on both coffee and tea, as well as paper towels, and should probably pick up a fresh bag of Akeyla-friendly apples.

My canine emperor barked.

Across the lake, someone yelled. Another boom followed.

I should also stop at The Great Hall and speak to Arne or Dag. Ask them about the recent uptick in new building permits.

"Perhaps they will do me the courtesy of a consultation before selling the next lot, huh, boy?" I said.

Marcus Aurelius barked again.

The noise of the construction tapered off as I made my way across the clover and acorns toward the garage. The canopy of Lizzy's oak towered over the smaller, younger birch and aspen around the house. The garage was also tucked between two other large oaks. Squirrels chirped and birds sang. I watched my footing as I always did, so I didn't poke my foot on a particularly hard nut, or roll my ankle on a hidden rock.

Two hundred years of remade life, and to this day, I still sometimes fumbled or missed a mark. Two hundred years of life with elegant and graceful elves and yet I continued to lumber on legs that were not truly my own.

Daily practice helped. I painted for a while, then briefly took up the violin. Target practice with a bow or a rifle came easier, and I was now a decent shot. But dancing never happened, and even though I can handle a sewing machine, I've always had to rely on the elves for tailoring.

Fine or gross motor skills, neither have ever matched the speed or strength my maker baked into my piecemeal body.

A crow cawed close by, but from which tree my piecemeal senses did not tell me.

The brambles moved.

There, hidden in the shadows among the stand behind the garage, were a white snout and two distinctive black-rimmed bright-blue hound eyes.

Sled dog eyes. *Lizzy's* eyes.

"Marcus Aurelius," I said, "do you see her?"

Lizzy ducked her head. The blue of her eyes flickered and trailed through the shadows as if she pulled a hot flame behind her.

My living hound whined and cocked his head as if listening. He obviously did not smell our visitor, nor, it seemed, did he see or sense her in any way.

Yet she watched me. "Lizzy?" I called.

She vanished into the shadows. The brambles rustled, and the branch swayed as she pulled back her head.

My Lizzy was not a phantom.

"Come, girl!" I yelled. How was this possible?

I lived among elves. I was familiar with magic. I'd come face-to-face with ghosts and spirits many times in my long life. I'd witnessed the making of many and the culling of more. I understood what they were and how they came about.

But this apparition was unlike any I'd seen before.

I quickly rolled up my sleeve. Magic and I have an understanding —I let it be and it doesn't explode in my creature-of-science face—but it was kind enough to allow me to wield enchantments gifted by others.

The tracers tattooed on my forearm shimmered blue-violet and green. I flipped my arm out, and pointed.

Nothing. A tracer lifted off my scarred inner arm and danced as a prismatic heat mirage above my skin, but it did not follow. It, like Marcus Aurelius, sensed nothing that needed following.

I looked back at the bramble. It had moved. I saw it move. Perhaps a squirrel? But Marcus Aurelius chased every squirrel that dared to set foot in the clover.

I knew what I saw. It may have been two centuries, but I knew my Lizzy—even if her eyes had flickered like flame.

I also knew what time of the year it was. The veil always thinned around Samhain, even a full moon beforehand. Thinned and let through spells and phantoms.

Here I stood, the semi-corpse *jotunn* able to see magic. I saw the workings of the tracer enchantments on my arms, and the protection marks along the side of my scalp when they lifted off my body to do their work. The marks that, more than anything else, told the magicals of the world that I was under the protection of the elves of New World Alfheim.

But Lizzy felt different—*looked* different. How, I could not quite say. More solid? Less solid? She left no traces of any real magic. No shimmers on the brambles, or a good fright in the gut of my living dog.

Perhaps I imagined her. Perhaps the true magic here was my mind making a representation of my life before the intrusion of intolerable neighbors.

Or maybe this was magic I did not know. New magic. Perhaps the magic of creepily persistent spells of creepy exes? "Come, my emperor," I said. I needed to know. "Time to see an elf about a dog, huh?"

My living hound barked reassuringly and followed me to the truck.

Time to visit the Elf King of Alfheim, Arne Odinsson.

CHAPTER 4

Alfheim proper covered about fifteen square miles of territory, with commercial and retail districts spilling out along the highway. One or two squat apartment buildings hid in the trees along the side roads. The state-run community college sat on a hill north of the city. But mostly the town stayed confined to its ancestral lands.

Except the old Ramsey Mansion. No one knew why the family who once owned the land named the manor after Minnesota's First Territorial Governor, Alexander Ramsey—Alfheim was too far north for the Ramsey family to have cared during Minnesota's formative years. But by the time I returned from the Civil War, the massive stone mansion had been built on yet another hill overlooking the elves' lands. The mundanes responsible abandoned it shortly thereafter.

Now the Ramsey Mansion was a tourist attraction on the way into town. It was also Alfheim's one and only branch library—and home to the town's two vampires, Tony and Ivan Biterson.

Their names weren't really Tony and Ivan, and they most certainly were not born as Bitersons. The elves can be a bit... sarcastic, and I'd long suspected that the name was one of Arne's many ways of keeping the two vampires under his control.

Tony and Ivan were as different as night and day, but both seemed inclined to behave themselves. Rumor was that they had both been Russian Cold War spies—which I did not believe for one second. But Arne had found the claim entertaining and had given them a job when they first showed up in the fifties. One they enjoyed. They sorted and organized the less-than-savory papers left behind by Alfheim's one and only witch, Rose.

Not many individuals could touch her darker notebooks and artifacts. A few of the elves could, but witch magic corrupted, and no one deemed Rose a witch of enough note to make the risk of corruption worthwhile. I could, but Arne long ago decided that he would not inflict such a painful trauma onto me.

Rose's death had been hard enough.

The Ramsey Mansion was just off the highway on the way into town. I could stop. Ask Tony or Ivan if Alfheim's Special Collection held any scraps about fire spirits and ghosts. Rose horded everything —bones, bedlam, spells and enchantments—so I might not be grasping at straws.

Or perhaps one of the vampires had insight. Not that I would share my moment with Lizzy with a vampire. They sucked on more than just blood; they also sucked away energy and information.

Tony and Ivan might have been the nicest, sweetest, most lovingly-tough Russian spies to ever walk a dark Moscow night while they were alive, but they were effectively dual personalities now. In those undead bodies lived both the intelligent men of mystery and their psychotic killer shadow-selves.

I parked my truck under a tree in the small lot cut into the side of the hill below the mansion. I patted Marcus Aurelius's head as I fully rolled down all the windows. He'd have a good cross breeze and could jump out if he needed to. "Watch the truck," I said.

He thumped his tail on the seat and laid down his head. He'd snooze while I chatted with our blood-sucking neighbors.

Sunlight sliced into the lobby as I swung open the doors. It arched across the tile toward the eight inlaid lines: each solstice and equinox, plus the four seasonal midpoints, Samhain included.

The lines served to educate the children of Alfheim's mundane population. For Tony and Ivan, they were the outer edges of their daylight cage.

The entire foyer and ballroom of the mansion had been stripped out, opened up, and filled with shadow-producing book racks. Tall, high, shaded windows allowed in indirect sunlight for the patrons, most of which fell on the children's play area. It also formed a shadowed trail through the daylight for Tony and Ivan.

The huge round librarian desk sat in the center front of the room just off the door-edge of their sunlight cage. A decorative roof of Norse-inspired scrollwork sheltered the desk from the windows.

A massive bouquet full of tropical flowers sat to one side. Maura hadn't said anything about donating to the libraries, but that didn't mean Sam wasn't sending the flowers over.

I stared at the damned thing for a long moment, until Tony cleared his throat.

Tony sat behind the desk, his feet propped up and his phone in his hand. He wore one of his many Alfheim County Library t-shirts, this one a dusty deep red that added a rosy tint to his too-alabaster skin and a hint of fire to his glossy, almost-Medusa-like curls.

In life, Tony Biterson had been a sweet-looking twenty-something with strong-if-young features, warm, honey-colored eyes, a straight nose, and a wide, charming smile. He stood nose-to-nose with Arne, which put him over six feet, and he carried himself well with wide shoulders and a slim, athletic build.

Now, he worked the con favored by the modern undead: the handsome-if-scary boyfriend with a semi-criminal side who needed a good taming. Being a librarian added a dash of nerd. Tony played the part well.

Tony looked up as I walked toward the desk. The blue light from his phone screen caught in his preternatural eyes, and for a split second they shimmered as if infested with magic.

Then he grinned.

Elves, when angry and out of their glamour, can be terrifying, but even Arne's ire paled in comparison to the shiver Tony generated.

Inside that loveliness and behind that handsome face beat no heart. Blood circulated only by the sheer will of the vampire's addiction to stealing more. Muscles moved, but in a shadowy, slippery way.

Like his skin, his teeth were too bright and too alabaster. Too clean. Too predatory.

Tony dropped his feet off his desk. "What can I do you for today, Mr. Victorsson?" He tucked his phone into the back pocket of his jeans. "Got some good odds on the Gopher football game tonight, if you're interested."

Tony and Ivan ran the Ramsey library branch. They also ran bets. And the extra special accounts of some of the local shipping businesses. Arne let them because, he said, "A little naughtiness helps them keep their larger evils under control."

"Not today," I said.

Tony walked over to the customer counter. He ran his hand over one of the bouquet's oversized red blossoms, then sniffed a smaller, yellow orchid. "Donated," he said. "Nice, aren't they?"

"Quite," I said.

Tony signed into the computer. "Got a handful of new bodice-rippers in yesterday." He pointed over his shoulder. "Looks like a few of them haven't been checked out yet."

He grinned again.

"Enough, Tony," I growled.

The grin vanished. "You're not going to break a window and finish me off, are you?" He batted his lovely eyelashes.

I couldn't tell if he was serious or continuing his smart-ass ways.

"Again," I said, "not today."

His eyebrows arched. "Good, good." Then he tapped absently at his keyboard. "Then I'll assume you're here because you're looking to enjoy an afternoon amongst the Rare Collections?"

"Yes," I said.

Tony shrugged. "Ivan's down there now."

Of course Ivan was in the basement with the witch papers. Ivan was Tony's opposite—short, squat, and troll-like—which was why Tony did most of the human meet-and-greet.

I turned toward the back stairwell.

"Mr. Victorsson," Tony called.

He stood perfectly still behind the librarian desk, a might-be ex-Russian spy who ran bets and sucked the blood of the innocent. "Samhain's coming," he said, then slid back into the shadows.

CHAPTER 5

No natural light filtered into the Ramsey House basement. What windows had been built into the mansion had been shuttered with steel casings for "environmental control," and unless they had an inspection, Ivan and Tony preferred candles to overhead fluorescents or halogens.

A front antechamber at the base of the stairs showcased several of the House's Victorian features, including the boiler and the massive, wood-fired stove. The house even had a cheese cave.

Behind the tourists' room, a modern mechanical room housed the gas furnace, water supply, and access to the duct work.

The Rare Collections room was hidden behind a wall of wires and ducts, half of which were non-functional and there only to confuse mundanes. I ducked under a pipe and twisted so I could wiggle behind the furnace, and scrunched down to pass through the low, claustrophobic door.

The hidden half of the basement extended beyond the house's foundations and out to the curved rock wall that supported the grand balcony overlooking the mansion's gardens. Above us, rich mundanes used to dance under the moon, inside and outside the wall of flung-open doors. Down here, the rocks poked out from the walls the way they would in any cave.

Earth oozed here, between the joints of the rocks, and cooled the entire space. The air was surprisingly dry, though close and heavy.

Ivan looked up from his tilted draftsman's desk. The flickering candles at either side of his project tossed orange light onto his sallow, pale skin. Reds danced in his deep-set dark eyes. Long ago, a creature had managed to permanently scar his left cheek, and when he grinned, the right side of his face lifted more than the left.

At times, Ivan reminded me too much of my younger self, with the ugly skin and the scars.

He hopped off his stool. Ivan stood a good foot shorter than Tony, but was wider at the shoulders. He hadn't been handsome in life, and his transformation into one of the undead had not given him the same statuesque quality it had given Tony.

But it did make him stealthier. Ivan blended into the environment. Perhaps it was a consequence of his vampire enthrallings. Perhaps he just looked more like the rock. But Ivan was not always noticeable.

"Mr. Victorsson," Ivan hissed. Over seventy years in Alfheim and he still carried just enough of his odd, indeterminate Eastern European accent to add a hint of snake to his words.

"Ivan," I said. I may not like the vampires, but I had enough respect to never refer to them as Biterson to their faces.

He patted the angled top of his desk and the propped-up, open manuscript it held. "Samhain?" he said.

Ivan did not ask questions. Ivan used questions to inform you that he already knew the answers you sought.

Samhain was a night of everything and nothing, of life and death, of love and hate. A witch had to understand the power of Samhain, and her own conductivity, and what she could channel.

Elves, fae, and especially their Japanese kin, the kami, controlled magic in its most natural state. Witches, because of their mundane blood, resisted the flow. And like all resistors, they corrupted and overheated.

Rose had overheated. Mentally, physically, magically. She overheated and her house burned and Ivan the vampire was now the only individual with enough corruption in his soul to be able to make sense of her corrupted, crazy rantings.

Ivan, and me.

"Samhain and long-distance spells," I said.

Ivan puckered his lips and tapped his temple. "Portals? Gates?"

I held my body language. Ivan's ability to read the nature of the moment was as reptilian as his voice. He'd strike before you realized he had his fangs out.

"Fire," I said.

Ivan rounded his mouth. "*Ahhh....*" he breathed. "The blossoms?" Ivan bounced and held up his long, troll-like finger. "They smell of elf magic."

I clutched my hands behind my back and struck my best military pose. The two vampires responded to the local chain of command as much as any other magical in town. I might not be elf, but I was one of Arne's "favorites." Playing up my elven connection served me well at times.

Ivan, this time at least, did not seem impressed. "So much magic!" he giggled, and did a small, troll-like two-step.

I dropped the pitch of my voice. "And this surprises you how, Ivan?" I rumbled. "Every inch of Alfheim smells of elf magic."

He rounded his mouth again, then flashed a too-bright, death's-head grin. "Do you know what happens when you mix magicks, Mr. Victorsson?" He sniffed at the air as if inhaling the world's finest perfume.

Akeyla was what happened when you mixed magicks—a fire spirit elf with incredible promise.

Many of the older magicals had a problem with "mixing," Ivan and Tony among them. Akeyla got stares. Then again, so did I, even after two hundred years. I wasn't magic, but I was the ultimate example of the distasteful practice of mixing.

"Ivan," I said, "I find your attitude wanting."

He clicked his tongue and curled one of his long, bent fingers. "Yes, yes." He tapped the finger against the side of his nose. "But there is *mixing*, Mr. Victorsson." He flittered it through the air, then pointed it at his desk.

I walked over to the desk and the open leather-bound journal.

Nothing showed on the pages. No words. No diagrams or sketches. No poems written in Rose's blood or smudges made of the ash of burned bones.

No quotes. No wishes. No calls for help. Nothing.

I frowned.

Ivan leaned forward like the little troll-like vampire he was. "You no see?" he asked.

"What do *you* see?" He wouldn't tell me the truth. I could tell by the set of his undead shoulders.

"Ashes." He hissed out the final "s" like air escaping a tire.

I didn't take the bait. I waited.

He looked up at me, his face a mask of innocence. "Much of her end work involves boundaries of some type, Mr. Victorsson." He stepped back from the desk. "Samhain is one of the nights when magic dances on its edges. When steps move back and forth."

He did the two-step again.

Dancing. Mixing. Ashes.

"Samhain comes, so I do my diligence." Ivan nodded. "I always check her works of mixing at this time of the year. *Always.*"

He pointed at the notebook again, and again, he batted his troll-like eyes to feign innocence. "I know nothing of *your* questions, Mr. Victorsson, but I am *always* happy to help when I can."

Ivan grinned again.

"And you see this on a blank page?" I had been special to Rose, and she to me. She allowed me to see into her soul not because I was corrupted enough to match her—though I was corrupted by the death from which my father molded me. She allowed me to see because she trusted me.

Yet those blank pages said otherwise. Carefully, I flipped through the book.

All the pages were blank. "I don't remember an empty notebook among her saved artifacts."

Ivan pushed on the side of his nose, flattened his nostril, and inhaled through the other side. "It is what it is, Mr. Victorsson."

I slammed the notebook closed. The desk jerked and wobbled, and a low, humming vibration rumbled from its legs. The candles flickered.

I ran my finger over the tanned cowhide wrapping the book. It wasn't anything special. No tooled designs. No charms. No magic hummed off it, or rose like a shade. This book had simply been one of Rose's many depositories of her ramblings. It had never held a spell or an enchantment.

It was empty.

Ivan did not move. "Would you like to check out this volume, Mr. Victorsson?"

I felt his thrall-push. He wanted me to take it.

"Wrap it up for me, please, Ivan." I stepped back. "I will do my best to keep it safe."

CHAPTER 6

Ivan wrapped the notebook in brown paper and tied it with twine. I set it behind the passenger seat of my truck. Marcus Aurelius stared, but thankfully did not growl.

I couldn't take the book into The Great Hall. Nothing touched by witch magic could cross the glamour into elfdom. I pulled out my phone.

Arne's number went to voicemail. "Something's been bothering me," I said, and hung up. The less detail—and the less time on a cell phone—with Arne, the more likely I'd catch his attention.

Dag answered when I called her number. "Come by my office later," she said. "Maura and I are finishing up here." Then she hung up on me. She didn't like phones any more than her husband did.

I didn't bother with Maura. Her ex's latest attempt to win her back must have had something subtle attached to it, or she wouldn't have called in her mother.

Looked as if I was on my own for a couple of hours.

Marcus Aurelius wagged his tail.

"Should we stop at Lara's? Get our coffee and you a treat?" I could finish my shopping and then head over to Dag's office.

Lara's Café and Deli had been a mundane town staple for close to a century. The original Lara passed away in the early sixties from smoking too much, and the café passed to her nephew, who immediately sold it. It had changed hands every five years or so for the past several decades, but never closed, mostly I suspected because the elves liked it. The interior had a woodsy, dark grove feel.

Lara's occupied its own brick building in the center of a small parking lot, which made it easier to glamour, if an elf saw fit to do so. The huge elm shading the back of the building helped as well. More trees spread up the hill behind the building. Out front, the short driveway opened onto the main road leading through the center of Alfheim.

The café was now owned and operated by a Syrian family who had recently moved north from The Cities and who must have changed to new distributors. Lara's coffee and tea—and the pastries—had significantly improved since they took over.

I parked my truck and watched the café door for a long moment. Marcus Aurelius turned circles in the passenger seat, hoping to come in with me. "Sorry," I said. "You need to stay in the truck."

He yipped his dog equivalent of a frown.

"Do you not want to stay in the truck because of the book?" Perhaps I should put it in the tool chest in the truck's bed.

My dog yipped again.

"All right," I said, and pulled it out from behind the seat. Ivan had done a superb wrapping job. The midafternoon sun detailed the crisp corners and the perfectly tensioned string. "Perhaps Ivan should open a gift wrapping boutique, huh?"

Marcus Aurelius barked.

"You're right," I said. "Who wants a vampire wrapping their Christmas gifts? Takes a bite out of the holiday spirit, huh?"

My dog whined.

"The joke wasn't that bad," I said.

He looked away.

I chuckled. The book must not be putting off any undetectable horrors, otherwise there wouldn't be jokes, no matter how terrible.

"I'll get you a treat." The deli often had pet biscuits.

The entire front window of the café was decked out with painted-on apples. Alfheim's Apple Festival—the first of the season's pre-Samhain festivities—brought in tourists. It also gave the elves an excuse to party.

From the sign on the window, it looked as if Lara's was running a special on fritters.

I entered intending only to purchase coffee. I exited with a month's worth of Earl Grey, three pounds of coffee, a bag full of fritters, half an apple pie, and the promised special treat for Marcus Aurelius, who barked and stuck his head out the open window.

I patted his head. "Thank you for not jumping out and chasing squirrels."

The emperor barked again.

A couple of tourists had taken up spots at the tables by the door while I was inside. They sipped their coffee and tried not to obviously stare at my scars and head tattoos.

A familiar sedan pulled into the lot.

A golden wave of Akeyla's fire elf warmth spread out from Maura's car. Maura must have picked her up from school on her way from of the florist.

The little elf burst from the sedan's backseat. "Uncle Frank!" she squealed, and, as always, jumped into my arms.

I swung her up to my hip and did my best not to jostle her or my big bag of café goodies too much.

"Hey, Frank. Did we run out of coffee?" Maura asked. "Or tea?" She wagged her finger.

I laughed and wiggled Akeyla to settle her better on my hip. "I'm here to buy Marcus Aurelius treats." I held up my bag.

Akeyla pointed at my dog. "Why is he in there all by himself?"

"Because I was about to give him his treats," I said, and held up my bag again.

Akeyla frowned. "That's not a good reason."

Maura winked. "She's training to take over Dad's job," she said. "She's big on logic right now, aren't you, honey?"

Akeyla nodded her agreement. "You need to make sense when you answer someone's question, Uncle Frank. If you don't make sense, then you're ob… odd-fuss…" She frowned.

"Obfuscating?" I asked.

"Odd fussing," she answered.

Odd fussing was the best definition of *obfuscating* I'd heard in a long time.

"Are you a third grader or a grad student?" I asked.

Maura closed one eye and tapped her temple. "Odin grants us knowledge and magic," she said.

Odin, and her father, the man who called himself son of Odin. Arne had been the Elf King of Alfheim for a thousand years and wasn't likely to hand over his job no matter how capable his grand-daughter grew up to be.

Akeyla pointed at the café. "We're getting the macadamia nuts!"

Two crows on the roof cawed as if angry she wasn't going to share her bounty—or our brownies—with them.

Maura took Akeyla and set her down on the ground. "Give Marcus Aurelius his treats." She pointed at my truck. "We'll be home later. We're going to the Geroux's, aren't we?"

Akeyla bounced again. "Jax has a cold and didn't come to school and I have his homework." She pointed at the sedan. "I think he's faking." She frowned.

Akeyla was probably correct—werewolves rarely caught colds. But then again, Jax was a third grader, and kids were known disease vectors.

"Nice of you to bring him his studies," I said.

Akeyla patted my hand. "You talk like an old person, Uncle Frank."

Maura laughed and took Akeyla's hand. "Let's get our nuts, huh?"

"It's full moon this weekend and he *can't* be sick." Akeyla pointed at the sky. "It's almost feast time."

"You can always come to feast, Frank," Maura said.

The werewolves and the elves feasted together before every full moon. Gerard and Remy said it helped the pack attach to the elves' magic, which helped them hold onto their humanity while in wolf form.

And holding their humanity was of the utmost importance with tourists around. With the elves' help, the Alfheim Pack hadn't killed a mundane in five decades, and even that kill had been disputed and likely self-defense on the part of the wolf involved. Before that, it had been almost a full century.

Gerard and Remy traveled the world and rescued the newly-turned. The good and strong-willed, like Gerard's wife, Axlam, were often brought to Alfheim. With the elves, the wolves could live full lives. Without the elves' magic to help them, Arne would have had to put down the entire pack long ago.

Or at least that's what Arne liked to claim. I figured as long as the arrangement worked for everyone, it was not my place to comment.

"I'll think about it," I said.

Maura gave me a quick hug. "You know you're always welcome."

"I know," I said. The elves always welcomed me. I was their adopted *jotunn*, after all. Like all Norse magical creatures, they liked their giants.

Maura took Akeyla's hand and they walked toward the café door. In my truck, Marcus Aurelius yipped. The two icy tourists continued to stare at me. One got out his phone. The two crows took flight.

"I'm coming, oh great emperor of mine." I opened the truck's door.

A sedan buzzed by on the road in front of the café. An ordinary sedan, one of boring metallic beige and boring, common rounded corners. It was one of those cars that unless you saw the emblem, you would have no idea of the make, much less the year.

The sedan slowed and for some internal reason, some inkling I did not understand, I looked over my shoulder at Maura and Akeyla as they stepped into Lara's Café.

When I looked back, the sedan had moved far enough along the road that it momentarily blocked the entrance to the parking lot.

Blocked the entrance and sat perfectly perpendicular to the café's door as Maura held it open for Akeyla.

Geometry mixes with magic. Geometry was one of the ways non-magicals called up spirits, or accidentally brewed an enchantment.

Geometry guided the protection glyphs on my scalp, and the tracers on my forearm.

The sedan had geometry and—

And my father. Victor Frankenstein leaned out of the passenger-side window, his cold, blue eyes gleaming like diamonds and his brown hair cut into the short, forward-pushed early-Nineteenth-Century style he preferred. Victor Frankenstein, the mad scientist whom I had left for dead on the Arctic ice two hundred years ago. Victor, the man who fashioned me from clay polluted by death.

Dead Victor Frankenstein. A ghost. A wraith, just like my Lizzy.

That Victor Frankenstein pointed at the café.

I looked back at the door just as the fireball blew out the front window.

CHAPTER 7

Marcus Aurelius was out the open door and bounding for the café before I dropped my bag on the seat.

The café door swung open. Maura pushed Akeyla out. "Take her!" she yelled, and disappeared back inside.

Akeyla screamed. Her glamour shattered. Flame-like magic erupted around her small body. The two tourists who had been staring at me earlier had already ducked into their car, and thankfully did not see Akeyla's ears.

"Akeyla!" I shouted. "Honey! Come here!" I took a step toward her.

Her lips rounded into a circle. She blinked, then screamed again.

My little niece *screamed*, and took off for the trees behind the building.

Marcus Aurelius barked at the broken café window, then barked at Akeyla. Thankfully, he paced her as she ran around the corner.

I looked back at the road. The sedan had vanished. Totally vanished, as if it had never been there. And my terrified, vulnerable, un-glamoured niece was running for the trees.

"Akeyla!" I yelled. I had to trust that Maura would get the owners and customers out on her own. I also had to trust that someone else would call the fire department.

I rounded the corner just as Akeyla climbed the small hill behind the café and disappeared into the stand of trees.

How did she get so far ahead? I might not be agile, but I was fast, at least when moving in a straight line. But Akeyla was already disappearing into the grove.

She couldn't get far. We might be on the outskirts of Alfheim, but we were still within its borders, and the buildings here were dense enough that she could not vanish.

I hoped.

But if I didn't hurry, I would lose her in the brambles.

Marcus Aurelius barked. "Stay with her!" I yelled. He would. He was a good dog.

Akeyla screamed again.

The birch tree directly in my path caught fire.

The entire thing, from its paper-white trunk to its drying yellow leaves, burst into flames like Moses's bush. Burst into a hot, blistering fireball not unlike the one that had rolled out of the café moments before.

Heat slapped my flesh and singed my eyes. I breathed in the crackle of exploding sap. And *fire* took over my senses.

Full fire. Real fire. Chaos and death and heat.

I do not do well when my skin reminds me that it is, in fact, alive. That I was not the corpse I thought myself to be. That I could die in a fire the way I lost the one friend I'd managed to make after my father fashioned me—the kind, blind man who had not understood the true monstrosity of my birth.

He had screamed like Akeyla screamed now.

I bellowed and blocked the flames with my arms.

The tree burned. The café burned. What if Maura died? What if Akeyla screamed until she was nothing more than a tiny elf-shaped cinder? Akeyla, my niece. The little girl I considered family. What if she lost her glamour forever?

My unsettled soul roiled. It boiled with the heat and it turned into a cauldron. I backed away. "Akeyla!" I yelled.

Somewhere on the other side of the fire, Marcus Aurelius barked. I couldn't... I couldn't get through. I couldn't walk through a wall of flame. No one could. No one.

A hand gripped my shoulder. "Frank!"

Arne Odinsson looked up at my face. Magic protected him. Magic stood between him and the chaotic flaming destruction in front of us.

Magic would save Akeyla.

"Did you put a tracer on my granddaughter?" he asked.

Flames whipped up into the air and took what little collected thought I had with them.

"Frank!" Arne checked my arm tattoos. "Did you at least see which way she went?"

"Marcus Aurelius is with her," I stammered. "They went up the hill."

Arne pushed me toward the lot. "Help Maura. I'll get Akeyla."

He dashed into the flames.

He dashed in, and I backed away.

ARNE HELD Akeyla against his chest. She tucked her head against his neck and sucked her thumb.

He held her because only he had the magic to glamour not only his own elfness, but also hers.

The fire department arrived within minutes, quickly extinguishing both the café fire and the tree. The café, the investigator was telling Arne, appeared to have had a gas leak in the kitchen. The blast had moved outward from the back of the building like a bubble bursting. Lara's cook had been in the walk-in refrigerator at the time and had come out of the ordeal in fine shape. The owner and two other customers were awake, talking, and in stable condition. Everyone was on their way to Alfheim's hospital to be more fully checked out. No one died. Everyone was expected to make a full recovery, Maura included, who the EMTs had taken in with the mundanes.

She'd saved the owner and gotten a bad burn on her arm while I ran away.

I leaned against my truck's not-so-glossy dark red fender. The exploding window had peppered my vehicle with shards of glass. If the emperor and I hadn't been behind the door, we would have been peppered, as well.

Marcus Aurelius sat on the passenger seat, his head down and his hound eyes wide. He'd led Arne to Akeyla.

She'd set fire to the tree. Simple magic swirled around its burned corpse like leaves blowing in the wind. The same magic flickered around the café. Akeyla's fire spirit side rained down on the parking lot like ash from a volcano.

Arne said nothing to the mundane firefighters or to Eduardo Martinez, Alfheim's sheriff. Of the first responders, only Ed had any real knowledge of magic.

Arne held his granddaughter and the mundane fire department saw a normal-looking, middle-aged, balding man in khakis and a buttoned-down shirt holding a clinging, frightened child. Arne's day-to-day glamour did nothing to disguise his broad shoulders and large arms, but it did make a mundane believe that he was past his peak. His days of fights and brawling looked to be long gone, but he somehow managed to hold onto his overall fitness as he aged.

Retired, Arne was not. Nor was he past his peak. No, Arne was King.

Akeyla was his wayward daughter's precious little girl who melted Arne's town-father heart. Sometimes I wondered if his displays of affection for his granddaughter were calculated to maximize public perception.

If they were, would it matter? He obviously loved her, no matter how he used her for political gain, or protected her from investigations.

I rubbed the sole of my boot through the parking lot's gravel, wondering if my ghosts were here to remind me of my weaknesses. I couldn't run around a burning tree to save her, or to help her deal with what had just happened.

The ghosts left no traces. Arne sensed no magic beyond Akeyla's young fire. I saw nothing. My tracers pointed toward the elves, but nothing else.

Perhaps I was simply seeing things.

Ed walked over. Alfheim County Sheriff's Department patrolled outside of town, and supported Alfheim's small internal police force. Ed was the de facto head of policing for the entire area, and everyone treated him as such, except for a few of the more annoying mundanes.

"Akeyla's safe," he said as he flipped through his notebook. "So is your dog." Ed was a good foot shorter than me, maybe a bit more. Almost all the elves were taller than him as well, though most of the wolves looked him in the eye. He was stout and wide-shouldered, and did not have an ounce of fat on him.

In many ways, he was a more-handsome, scaled-down, fatherly, Hispanic version of me. He, though, had only one scar and did not wear his hair elf-style, preferring the standard short cut of every cop everywhere.

I nodded.

"We're tracking down those two tourists." Ed nodded toward the road.

They had cell phones. Everyone had cell phones. The elves had to be careful.

"They ran off pretty fast," I said. As witnesses, they should have stuck around.

Ed sniffed as if reading my mind. He closed his notebook and tucked it into his pocket. "Tell me again what you saw."

Ed was one of the few people who credited my "seeing" magic, probably because he was a mundane. He did not wield magic, nor could he see it as I did. But he knew a lot about its effects.

Back in Texas, he'd had a run-in with a vampire serial killer, a nasty piece of work who enthralled victims so thoroughly that the elves' magic could not break the spell. I knew some of the story, mostly Arne's heroic tale of how he and three of the werewolves had gone down to help.

Because of its thrall, visually perceiving the evil thing had been nearly impossible, and hitting it with magic only made it more powerful.

Ed killed it. Not Arne or Remy. Ed, the mundane officer who was too good at his job to be wasting away here as sheriff, staked the vamp bastard and got the hamburger-like scar on his neck as his reward.

The putting away of his notebook said that he wanted to talk magic.

Should I tell him about the ghosts? Were they part of this or were they all me?

I didn't know.

"A ghost," I said.

Ed frowned. "What kind of ghost?" There were many. "What did it do? Did it use magic?"

It used fire, I thought, but I didn't say that to Ed. He knew. Maura knew. Arne knew, which was why he went up the hill to rescue Akeyla. They all knew fire was my weakness.

The more I thought about it, the more I suspected that ghosts were mine and mine alone, and were here to teach me a lesson.

"Nothing noticeable, or traceable." I shook my head. "I don't know, Ed. I don't know if the ghost is relevant to anyone other than me. My enchantments didn't consider the other ghost I saw this morning worth tracing." I held out my arm.

"Other ghost?"

"Both were people important to me a long time ago." Lizzy was as much a person as Marcus Aurelius. They were simple dog people.

"This was the second ghost you've seen today?" His frown deepened. "Do you think they're malevolent?"

"I don't know." Lizzy, no. But my father?

How much of my remembered rage from my newborn years colored how I saw my father? If he were alive and I met him now, would I have more empathy for his misguided attempts to control life? I've long wondered, if he had been older and less rash, would he have thought through his experiments instead of blundering into the misshapen pain that was me?

Or not. He did frame me for the murder of his fiancée, Elizabeth.

I have blundered, but I have never murdered.

My father's ghost could have been a warning. He could have been a haunting. Or he could have been malevolent.

The explosion could have been an Akeyla-caused gas leak. From the way Arne glamoured Akeyla, I suspected Arne thought so.

I traced out in the air the hand movements of my father's ghost. "He could have been telling me to attend to the fireball."

Or my weaknesses.

"This is the time of year when ghosts show up," Ed said absently. "Though they're a bit early, no?"

I didn't chuckle. I wasn't in a chuckling mood.

Or perhaps Ivan was correct: Now was the time of boundaries crossed. Of magicks mixed. Of forces that do not usually tangle suddenly knotting into fiery explosions.

My ghosts could be a tangential side effect of something very different.

Ghosts. Fire. Bouquets. "I can't help but wonder if Akeyla's father has something to do with all this."

Ed watched Arne rock Akeyla. "Yeah. Me too."

"I picked up a sense of geometry with the second ghost," I told Ed. "No actual magic. No overt malevolence." I had no idea how overtly Hawaiian magic swam with arcs and angles.

I glanced at my truck. Perhaps Rose's vanished magic held hints.

Arne rubbed Akeyla's back and she closed her eyes, but continued to suck her thumb even though she was eight. Even though I hadn't seen her revert to such self-soothing the entire time she'd lived in Alfheim.

The fire inspector nodded and walked off, leaving Alfheim's chief elf alone with his fire starter granddaughter.

Akeyla would know what the adults thought of her. She picked up on everyone's attitude. Akeyla always picked up on subtle energy that everyone else missed.

Sort of like me.

Ed adjusted his hat. "Her father's a fire spirit, correct?" Ed rubbed his cheek.

An edge to his voice added a hint of accusation to his words.

"He can't leave his island," I said. "Neither Akeyla nor her father had anything to do with the explosion, Ed. It was a gas leak. She's frightened. That's all."

He straightened his belt. "I hope you're right."

So did I. But what, exactly, was *my* father's ghost trying to tell me?

"Do you want me to come by your place?" Ed asked. "To look at the brambles?"

"No," I said. "It's fine."

"Are you sure?"

"I'm sure, Ed."

Ed nodded. "If you have any trouble, call it in, okay?"

"I will." Most of his deputies were mundanes who had no clue about Alfheim's true natures. A few did. One was a werewolf. We all knew who to call if we needed police help.

I watched as Ed walked over to Arne.

Arne Odinsson, the true Alpha of the elves, werewolves, and other creatures who lived in Alfheim, myself included.

Ed pointed at the burned tree. Arne raised his hand. "We'll deal with it," he said. *We*, meaning the elves.

Ed did not look happy.

"I'll take her to see her mother," Arne said, and turned his back not only on Ed, but also on me.

Arne Odinsson, the elf whom in many ways I considered my adoptive father, turned his back and walked away with my niece in his arms.

CHAPTER 8

Lizzy's cairn glowed in the evening sun. Reds and bold oranges caught in the agate, and golds warmed the gray lakeshore stones.

I ran my finger over the marker's granite base. "What were you trying to tell me, girl?"

Weakness, I thought. Unsettled and monstrous weakness.

Two hundred years ago, my father called me "demon." My father, a man of lesser morals and tainted ethics, dropped at my feet those two syllables of truth in which I now wrap myself.

Two hundred years ago, we stood on opposite sides of a widening crack in the Arctic ice. He yelled his slur from a face buried deep within his wolf-trimmed hood. He clenched his fists and stomped his black seal-skin boots.

His eyes gleamed inside the shadows under the fur, like blue jewels forged in the fires of Hell itself.

The slick ice rocked under our feet. My dogs howled; his lay as a dead, broken heap of cooling meat. The floe groaned and the wind ground across my exposed flesh more like burning nettles than the shimmering, swirling snow it was.

We both breathed in the air at the dawn of the Industrial Age, my father and I. We both inhaled the crisp, shattered cold and we both exhaled the soot of our souls. He breathed by virtue of birth. Me, by an unholy gift I still do not comprehend.

"Demon!" my father shouted as he pointed his finger at my chest.

My father, the man who made my savage body and forged the equally savage geometry of my soul.

The cold bothered me little, though it tore and cracked my dogs' paws, Lizzy's included. My skin had already proven itself both tough and near-indestructible.

Perhaps I was a demon. My father demanded that I cinch that word tight around my neck. Perhaps he was correct.

Perhaps the trail of death left in our wake was more caused by me than him, as he claimed. Perhaps I had no reason to lay chase when he fled across the frozen waste of the North. Perhaps his feigned innocence was not feigned.

I bellowed and slammed my foot into the shattering ice, and between my father and I, the Arctic Ocean welted as slushy, slow, iron-gray waves. My dogs backed away, and carried my sled with them.

The berg under my father's feet tipped. Shock sparked his blue eyes. He swung his arms to hold his balance, but the ice found no reason to agree.

My father fell hard on his arse. My dogs barked.

I took his immaculate word of strangulation, that label of demon, from my father. I allowed it to boil. I was rage. I was pain.

And I allowed it to make me little more than the demon he claimed.

My ice floated away, but my anger did not. My father turned tail and ran.

My dogs growled, as did I.

I gripped my sled's reins. The dogs did not care if I bled hellfire; they only wished to run.

We drifted along the ice after that, a demon and his four-legged hounds, out in the biting air and under the blistered, gray-blue sky.

My father's threats and insults vanished into the screams of the Arctic wind. He all but disappeared into the haze.

I had vowed vengeance. Instead, I found a colony of elves in the center of a far-flung continent. I buried my Lizzy. Within a decade, the elves found evidence of my father's befitting death in the slums of London. And I learned to organize the chaos of my soul.

But now I wondered if my chaos and my demonic nature called up ghosts.

Two hundred years into my immortal life and I should know better than to allow such thoughts and memories to cloud my mind. I had seen my share of death. I'd fought alongside Union soldiers during the Civil War. I'd seen villages burn. I understood hauntings.

Most ghosts manifested out of rage, or love, or shock. They were the final geometry of a soul, its final alignment with the universe, and they tended to sort order from the chaotic intensity of a final, emotional moment.

Hauntings weren't about good and evil. They weren't about a future beyond learning from your past.

I rubbed my forehead. My past was littered with lessons, but which ones applied to my future? The ghostly ones of Lizzy and my father?

Or, perhaps, the hidden ones of magicks mixed and boundaries crossed, and of the other kind of ghost I carried.

The tracers on my arms came from the elves, Dagrun in particular. The protection enchantments on my scalp, from Arne. I carried their enchantments for a reason.

A witch reason.

Not all witches walked the world with a black heart. Some started pure. Some fought the blackness with their last, dying breath.

Rose had been a witch with a pure-but-chaotic soul. She'd also been family.

Adoptive family, but not like the elves.

I found Rose and three other children in a Louisiana bayou shack surrounded by snakes and alligators. I'd been a soldier for close to five years at that point, and had fought many Union battles that had murdered better men than I. I flinched a lot. I think my mind wanted me dead, but my immortal body kept walking anyway.

In the bayou, the witch who'd kidnapped the children cackled under a full moon, and spewed a fountain of corrupted magic high into the air.

I fought her, I think, out of dread more than any other reason. Dread that I had survived the Civil War and so many others had not. Dread that I could no longer ignore the immortality of my body, or what it meant. Dread that I knew I needed to return to the elves and ask Arne for the same help with living that he gave the werewolves.

That witch, in that bayou under that full moon, had been meant to be my suicide by magic.

Instead, the witch took three of the four children with her into oblivion. I snatched Rose up and placed her on my hip. And together, we walked the banks of the Mississippi until we wandered, once again, into Alfheim, Minnesota.

For a time, she called herself Rose Franksdottir. Then the witch-twisting of her mind began.

She talked to herself first. She heard voices, and hallucinated creatures that did not walk among the elves—gods with the heads of jackals or birds or gators, she said, though all of us were sure she had a pipeline into Egyptian mythos.

She took books, journals and other writing materials, crystals, metals, clay, animals—anything and everything she found—into her house. Mostly, she stole. Objects went in, and Rose rarely came out.

My memories of many of those years after the war weren't well-formed. Many times, I considered another attempt at suicide by witch, since I had so graciously brought a witch into Alfheim. But I could not do that to my Rose, nor could I do that to the elves who, at the time, were trying to help her.

They would have killed her the moment she set foot in town if she'd come in with a mundane. But it had been my hand she held, so the elves held her hand, too.

I'd been drinking the night her house burned. It takes considerable amounts of high-proof liquor to have an effect on me, and at the time,

I'd been doing my best to figure out how much and how fast I needed to consume in order to black out.

I remember the screams more than anything else. The animals, the elves, the house, Rose. I remember the flames and I remember being as paralyzed by the heat and the brightness as I was behind the café.

Rose had enchanted the house. No elf could come close then, and they couldn't now.

Only me.

I had stood on the edge of the magic circling her small cottage and watched a good-if-tormented soul burn. I watched the chaos of her mind become the chaos of her world. She died in that blaze. Rose became dust.

Now, I walked the garden path around my cabin to my lake-facing deck, and glanced at the wide French doors of my home. Rose had loved my cabin. She'd loved the lake, though she'd refused to leave her hill in her last few years.

Hammers echoed across the water. The neighbor's workers were finishing up for the day. I closed my eyes.

I carried more than elven magic. I carried Rose magic, too. Wispy magic so faint the elves paid no heed. Magic I could only see if I squinted.

It was, in its own way, another kind of ghost. Rose's imprint on my soul was the vestigial remains of my lone, failed attempt at building my own family. I shook my head and opened my eyes. The sun set behind the neighbor's glass and chrome behemoth and all the colors of Samhain danced in its windows. The workers by the shore laughed. Others drove home to their families.

Marcus Aurelius nuzzled my hand.

"Hey," I said, and rubbed his ear. He never liked my moods.

Neither did I. Two hundred years past the rage of my undignified re-birth and I still had difficulty regulating my emotions.

My dogs never judged.

I looked toward the forest-side of my house and Lizzy's cairn while I rubbed my hound's ears. "I am confused, my canine emperor," I grumbled. "I don't like being confused."

45

He whined and sat on my foot.

How could I not smile? "You do Lizzy proud, my friend."

Marcus Aurelius barked and padded off toward the French doors.

Why had I not yet found some comprehension of the day's events? What, exactly, were we mixing up here in Alfheim? At least Akeyla was safe.

I opened Rose's book one last time, as the sun dropped toward the horizon, wondering if it would reveal its secrets at the point of the sun's crossings.

Nothing. Only blank pages. I re-wrapped it and returned it to its place in my truck's toolbox. A part of me said not to bring it into my home. The rest of me agreed.

Rose had been eight when I brought her to town. For about a decade after her death, I'd see her dancing in the woods as if the fire had burned away what ailed her. Her ghost had realigned itself to the universe and my dear Rose had found peace.

Her phantom never varied. She twirled and she smiled, and she held out her hand. Then she vanished into whatever magic from whence she'd come.

That echo of Rose had bounced that way through my life for ten years, until she became too faint and finally evaporated for good. All that remained was the ashes of her house and her wisps in my soul.

The neighbor's unholy saws screeched across the lake. The cacophony provided some usefulness—it pulled my mind from my past "lessons" and drove away all thoughts of demons, fatherly, witchy, or otherwise.

Time to attend to the present.

Today's crew looked to have installed solar shingles. At least my noisy neighbors were environmentally conscious.

My phone rang.

Maura, my phone's screen said. She was probably calling to tell me that Akeyla would be spending the night at Arne's. I answered.

"I…" she said, then sniffled.

"Maura?" Was she hurt worse than she let on at the café? Was Akeyla hurt? And I hadn't helped. I ran when the fire became too hot.

46

"Frank," she sniffled again. "I just wanted to say that you will always be my big brother."

Maura had been born while I was experimenting with a college life in the sixties. She'd been a child about the same age as Akeyla when I returned to Alfheim.

She'd been my joy. Her smile, like her daughter's, helped me search for something beyond the darker moments of my life.

"What's wrong?" I asked.

"Those two tourists at the café? The two outside?"

Oh, no, I thought. I should have gone after them. I should have hit them with tracers so that Arne or Dag could track them down and take their phones.

But I didn't. I let Maura down. I let Arne down. Damn it, I let Akeyla down. And now video of elven magic was free in the world.

"Mom's taking care of it," she said.

Part of me felt sorry for the two tourists.

"There are rules, Frank," Maura said.

Yes, there were rules. Rules that protected the entire community. Rules that kept all of us safe while allowing Alfheim to continue to grow. Rules that applied to everyone, royalty or not.

That did not mean I had to like it.

"Akeyla needs guidance with her fire abilities," Maura said. She sounded as if she was attempting to convince herself more than me. "We're going back to Hawaii."

"You left for a reason," I said. Growled, actually. I'd seen the damage to her magic. The heat her ex had added.

She'd finally healed.

"Did you see anything at the café, Frank? Any other magic?"

"Other than the ghost?" I'd told Ed about my father and I was sure that Arne knew.

"Yes." She all but whispered.

Had I? "I don't know," I said. Though I should know.

"Akeyla didn't start that fire," she said.

All evidence pointed toward the opposite, and now the two tourists had video proof.

It all seemed too... clean.

"No," I said. "No, she didn't."

Clean and geometrical.

"We..." Maura sighed. "It's decided."

How the hell could it be decided? She was the Elf Princess of Alfheim. Didn't that count for something? What about Akeyla? Why had Arne made his decision so quickly? "Maura..."

"I gotta go. We'll be by to pack tomorrow." She sighed again, this time to cover a hiccup.

Was Arne really sending his daughter away? "I'll talk to your father. I'll leave now." I had to. Someone had to talk sense into Arne Odinsson.

"It's been decided. There's nothing you can do."

"I don't care."

"Frank..."

"Maura, it's the least I can do. Let me do this. Please."

After a pause, she answered. "Okay. Thank you."

She ended the call. I stared at my phone. Should I call Arne? My gut told me no. Better to stand face-to-face with Alfheim's King. But I needed information.

Instead of calling Arne, I called the Queen of Alfheim. I called Dag.

"I'm in my office," she said, and hung up.

I tucked my phone into my pocket. Time for me to walk into that fire.

CHAPTER 9

Alfheim's City Administrative Complex—the elves refuse to call anything other than their Great Hall a "hall"—was a well-landscaped sprawling line of concrete and brick bunkers on the edge of town. Built in the early nineties during one of Minnesota's better municipal funding periods, the Admin Complex housed all of the city's mundane functions: police, fire, city and county officials, community center, main library, and the local county courthouse. We even had a kids' indoor playground, a gym, and a pool.

I parked my truck toward the back of the lot and away from the main admin building, and left Marcus Aurelius to his guard duty. Time for me to speak to the one elf in Alfheim capable of blocking Maura and Akeyla's banishment: Maura's mother, Dagrun Tyrsdottir.

My truck clicked and groaned as it cooled. I stared at the building, my body also clicking and groaning. My neck hurt. My back knotted. My fingers ached.

My demi-health crept up on me while my mind circled other thoughts and now decided to remind me that even though I was as immortal as the more powerful of the elves, I would never be as agile or alive. I unclenched my hands and slowly shook out the stiffness.

The world spun.

Right there on the concrete walk to the doors of the Admin Building, out in the open, my demi-health and my uncertainty whipped up a bout of vertigo.

For a second, a tornado touched down in my head and my life's geometry became arcs and curves. My life folded back onto itself. Responses I'd left behind—anger and vengeance that boiled over into a red, roiling rage—lifted up out of the holes in my soul. My arteries constricted and made my heart thump. My vision closed into a tunnel.

I knew this unsettled rage. My body remembered each time it broke through and inflicted itself onto the world: My father's attempts to destroy me. The Confederate soldiers who raped and murdered. Rose, at her and for her. The laughter of the mundanes. Each and every death of every one of my dogs.

My hauntings included more than ghosts.

I gulped in air and looked up at the early evening sky. *Count*, I thought. *Breathe.*

Trees rustled. Somewhere close by, a crow cawed. Warmth wafted up from the concrete under my feet. Cars moved in and around the lots, as did their exhaust.

I was not alone, no matter how lonely my thoughts made me. The world buzzed in the here and now.

A car honked. A young mother on the other side of the lot herded her children toward the community center.

The rage vanished. I inhaled deeply and slowly, and carefully exhaled.

Every day, I practiced attending to my body and my functions. I warmed myself in the sun and I drank my tea. I lived a quiet life with no place—or need—for rage. So why had it surfaced?

I shook my head and blinked.

A crow jumped from a tree near the building to the roof. It bobbed its head and spread its wings, and cawed again. Then it lifted its beak to the sky as if to say that the Aesir wanted me to pay attention.

"Which are you?" I asked. Huginn or Muninn, Odin's ravens of thought and memory, though this bird was neither Odin's nor a raven.

The crow cackled and stomped its bird foot. Then it too took wing toward the sunset.

I watched it fly off. Was it an omen? Warning? A bird entertained by the foibles of mundanes and magicals alike? Because if I was going to be laughed at by an animal, it would be a crow.

I shook my head. The best I could do now was to make my way toward Mayor Tyrsdottir's utilitarian outer office. Maura and Akeyla took precedent.

The reception desk for the entire town governance office sat behind a fish bowl of a glass wall and looked out over a boring hallway through which other office staff walked. Behind the receptionist and around a corner, Dag's office door was closed.

Dag was in there; magic filtered out around the jamb and along the carpet.

Dag's office manager looked up from her computer. Sue Martenson was a mundane who had married into the Alfheim Werewolf Pack and understood the true nature of magicals.

"Hi, Sue," I said.

She frowned, then nodded.

"Mr. Victorsson, how are ya today?" she said in her thick Northern Minnesota accent. The entire pack other than Gerard and Remy referred to me as Mr. Victorsson. I never did figure out why.

"Good, good. The sun's out, yeah? No rain coming." I said. You had to follow the social rules in Alfheim, which meant starting a conversation with mild pleasantries about the weather. I learned long ago that if you did not acknowledge everyone's greater environment, it was assumed that you didn't care about the community. Such a faux pas opened a person to a storm of Minnesota Ice instead of the usual, happy Minnesota Nice.

Sue smiled.

"I need to talk to Dag."

The smile vanished. "She's on a call."

Yells echoed from her office. Sue nodded toward the door just as a bubble of magic pushed through the wood frame.

Dag was not happy.

Emotions were contagious. What if Dag's anger swirled up the rage again?

No, I would not be held prisoner by my own faults. I waved to Sue and walked around the reception desk. Sue made no move to argue or to stop me, though I suspected that if I had been a regular mundane, she would have told me to take a seat.

I knocked.

"I know it's you, Frank," Dag called.

Dagrun Tyrsdottir sat on the edge of her grand oak desk, one elegant leg dangling over the edge. She'd fully dropped her glamour.

The cell phone in her hand cast a flat, bluish shadow over her almond-shaped eyes and her exquisite, straight nose.

Like her husband, Dagrun Tyrsdottir's magic swirled around her like silk caught in a breeze, and like all elves, she was beautiful in ways no mundane person could match. The enchantment tattoos circling her scalp just above her ears flowed over onto her forehead and formed a shimmering semi-cornet of silver and gray-blue which, like my own tattoos, danced just off her skin like a heat mirage.

The tracer tattoos on the back of her hands and up the inside of her forearms shimmered in the same way, as did the silver and pewter clasped into her long, seemingly-alive, earth-black ponytail.

Dag's tracer enchantments appeared more solid than the ones I carried—the ones she'd gifted me in the decades after I returned from the Civil War with Rose in tow.

Rose was why Dag had gifted me the tracer enchantments. Rose was also the reason for the protection sigils around my scalp. I'd long resisted elven markings. The tattoos were visible to mundanes, and only added to my perceived scariness. I got enough stares as it was.

But I conceded after Rose. Best to be protected from witches.

Dag, like Arne, rarely dropped her glamour outside of the elves' Great Hall, the glamoured elf-space where they could walk free without worrying about mundane eyes. But today, she paced Alfheim's Mayor's Office in full elf splendor, right down to her linen tunic, leather pants, and thigh-high, black, built-for-running boots.

Her long bow and quiver leaned against the wall between the two windows.

Dag looked ready for a hunt.

She ran her finger over the edge of her grand, pristine oak desk, then looked at the tip as if she'd picked up sludge off a sea monster. Then she held out the phone.

"Watch," she said.

I took the phone and tapped the triangle to start the video.

The two tourists sat at the table in front of Lara's window. Most of the footage was them gossiping about women they knew in The Cities and making fun of their small town coffee. They caught Maura and Akeyla entering the café, and made predictably boorish comments about Maura. The one shooting decided to continue filming her through the window, and to continue his loutish voice-over.

The final fifteen seconds of the video was by far the most problematic.

Inside the café, Akeyla brightened. She stiffened, and her glamour popped like a balloon. Maura gasped and covered her daughter's ears, but she was too late. Akeyla's ears were clearly elven. Clearly pointed.

Maura's compensation produced visible distortions around her daughter. Magic visible to not only me, but to anyone watching the video.

The owner of the phone swore as the magic around Akeyla caught fire. He swore again and ran away just before the window exploded.

Dag stared at the back of the phone. "That call you heard when you came in?" She looked up.

I nodded.

"Maura's grandfather."

My gut clenched. Tyr Bragisson was the King of the Icelandic elves, and Dag's father. His call meant that the video had already gone international, and explained the swiftness of Arne's decision. If the other elf enclaves demanded action, Arne had little choice. "How many views?" I asked.

Dag closed her eyes. "Not many, thank Odin," she said. "My

husband coordinated a takedown." She put out her hand to take back the phone. "We're still looking for the two who posted it."

I paced across the room, doing my best to not seem imposing, even though Dag had never—would never—read my body language as threatening. She was my adoptive mother, and knew me well.

Other than the massive oak desk, the Mayor's Office was a utilitarian shell complete with metal shelving and flickering fluorescent lights. The walls were the beige of old snow—that crusty, slightly lichen-filled color of desolate landscapes that humans should leave alone. The rows of shelves along the inner wall only reflected light where they'd been nicked down to their aluminum frames, and were otherwise the dark grey of volcanic rocks.

The office might seem bland to a mundane's eyes, but to me, it conjured images of Dag's homeland, Iceland.

From Dag's pacing, I wondered how protected Maura was at the moment. Dag stopped in front of one of the windows, still fully out of her glamour.

I pointed, but didn't say anything.

She flicked her finger over the blinds and they snapped closed. "Has Arne told you what happened the last time the mundanes caught an uncontrolled glimpse of an elf's power?"

At last count, there were about twenty-five normal people in Alfheim whom the elves trusted. Most of them were connected to the werewolves. Ed knew, as did his wife. And me, though I wasn't normal by any means.

"No," I said.

Her ponytail swayed behind her head. "The mundane gathered warriors. They trapped the elf family. Burned them alive except for their daughter. The man used her magic to make himself king." She glanced at the door. "They had many children."

Elves did not have babies with normal humans. The outcome was bad. "But…" Quite bad.

Dag closed her eyes. "Every single witch in the British Isles is descended from those children. All of them." She tapped her desk again. "The mundanes *cannot* overrun Alfheim. We *cannot* be outed to the wider world. Imagine what they would do to us now, with their technology."

Nothing good. But how could sending Maura and Akeyla away help? "This wasn't Akeyla's fault," I said. "How is sending her back to her father going to protect anyone? If he caused this, you're giving him what he wants."

Dag watched me with her stone-gray eyes. "Maybe he did this. Maybe not." Her voice held no hint of condescension, though it did hold weariness. "No other elf enclave will take Maura and Akeyla because of the video." Dag's melodic, crisp—though slight—Icelandic accent made it difficult for her to disguise her undercurrents of emotion.

Or, more likely, she did not bother with people she considered family.

The Icelandic elves would not take Dag's daughter. Nor would the Norwegians. Nor the kami in Japan. And there was no way Dag would send her daughter to the Siberian elves or either of the new colonies in New Zealand and South Africa.

So back to Hawaii they went.

"I have a gut feeling," I said. How else could I describe what bothered me? My hauntings, Maura's instincts. Ivan's convoluted warnings. They pointed to something different.

Dag nodded as she sat on the edge of the desk. "In the old days, we would have killed those men for what they did and stopped the rumors there."

"In the old days, the mundanes would not have shown such disrespect."

She looked up at the ceiling. Slowly, she raised her arms and turned the inside of her forearms upward.

For one brief flash, her tracers glowed green-blue.

"My husband has made his judgement." She dropped her arms. "He had no other choice."

"I don't—"

"Frank." This time Dag's voice did hold admonishment. I was not to interfere in elf business.

"But—"

Someone knocked on the door.

Dag suddenly glamoured. Her ponytail vanished, as did her tattoos. Her linen and leathers became a blouse and khakis. She became the middle-aged matron of a small, Minnesota town. "Yes?" she said.

Ed poked in his head. "I'm sorry to bother you, ma'am, but I need to get a statement from Maura."

Dag nodded. "I will pass on your message." She waved him away.

Ed frowned. "Mayor Tyrsdottir, I understand there's family politics here, but if the reports aren't thorough, we could be risking reprisals if the two who shot that video decide to lawyer-up."

Dag's eyes narrowed. I didn't think she'd thought through the legal implications of the modern mundane world.

She didn't respond.

Ed placed his hat on his head. "At least pass on my request, ma'am. That's all I ask."

She waved him away again. Ed looked at me, then at Dag, nodded once, and closed the door behind as he left.

"There has to be another way," I said. What if the video followed Maura and Akeyla to Hawaii? They couldn't stay sequestered forever.

"They're at The Hall," Dag said. "Say your goodbyes." She waved me away, too.

CHAPTER 10

Like all things elvish, Alfheim's Hall was glamoured. Any mundane driving through town saw only a slightly rundown, early-eighties designed, three-story hotel with an attached large restaurant and meeting room complex. The entire structure appeared to be poured concrete and painted beige as an afterthought. A couple of unkempt bushes dotted the landscaping rock surrounding its foundation. More bushes braved the scattered small islands in the seemingly empty parking lot.

The overall effect was "Ignore and pass by."

The rest of Alfheim's open commercial districts—Center Square, Wolftown, and the artsy bed and breakfasts that have popped up around the college campus—carried other glamours, though Center Square attracted visitors more with its 1870's architecture and tourist-oriented trading posts than anything magical.

The Great Hall occupied a wedge of land between Center Square and the river. A trail ran along the banks, which mundanes biked and walked, but The Hall's glamour made it appear unwelcoming, and no one ventured into the parking lot.

Maura once told me that the elves could not truly see the glamours they built. That, for them, a glamour slid along their skin like a prickly piece of silk. Most of them shook when they walked through one—Maura called it "heebie jeebing"—though I have never in my two hundred years with the elves seen one visibly react. They were a warrior people, the elves. Traders and fighters—much like their Norse ancestors and gods—and did not show weakness.

I parked my truck in the real lot across the street from The Hall. I try to be courteous parking my one-ton vehicle, but tonight the small lot was full, and I slid in next to a boxy sedan. Gerard and Axlam's larger sedan sat in the corner next to Remy's smaller truck. Arne's fuel-efficient hybrid sat under the light in the center of the lot.

I must not be the only person who'd come to say goodbye to Maura and Akeyla.

I wiggled out and held my door for Marcus Aurelius, who bounded out to the street. He stopped at the curb with his big tail wagging, and looked over his shoulder. My dog waited for me to catch up.

"What do you think, boy?" I asked as I looked both ways before crossing into The Hall's glamour.

Marcus Aurelius barked.

"I suspect you are correct." I patted his head. "We will fix this." What else could we do? I was old enough that I knew a mistake when I saw one.

The emperor wagged his tail.

I scratched his ear. "You are utterly predictable, you know that?" My dog was hungry. "Axlam undoubtedly has a treat for you."

Every dog loved Axlam, and even most cats. Arne's lynx purred for her, and he otherwise sat on the back of Arne's chair and glowered at everyone within pouncing distance.

Marcus Aurelius barked again and bounded through the glamour veil.

No bounding for me. I swept my hands before me as if parting curtains.

The gesture wasn't necessary, but over the years, I'd found that orienting my body to the magic helped me to understand it better. Here, parting the "curtain." At home, "throwing" a tracer spell. The elves thought my movements odd, and at times laughable, but it worked for me.

I stepped through into a different world—or, more correctly, a more natural world.

The land around The Hall was still the same virgin forest that was here seven hundred years ago, when the elves' Norse mundanes first stepped foot on North America. Not exactly the same—the trees, plants, and animals continued to grow and change—but The Hall sat on a riverbank that was otherwise untouched by European humans. Arne's lynx lived here, as did deer, fox, ravens, snakes, and a pair of bald eagles. The fishing along the shore was especially good.

The land itself was considerably larger than its external glamour. The Hall was a good quarter mile from the veil.

The strongest of the elves' magic warped space, but on which side of the glamour, I did not know. Perhaps both. I was not privy to the specifics of the spell, or who placed it originally, though I suspected an organized effort by Alfheim's first elves. I knew only that each step through the veil surrounding The Hall was a blessing bestowed on me by a magic that shimmered with as much life as the blue jays flitting between the branches.

Marcus Aurelius and I started down the trail toward The Great Hall of Alfheim.

No squirrel distracted my hound, and he trotted ahead. The birds inside the veil sang louder than the birds outside, and with more melody. More critters scurried between brambles and bushes. The evening sky here was also a deeper, richer, indigo blue, and I often wondered if the place behind the veil was Vídbláin, the Wide-blue heaven of the Eddic poems. Arne only grinned when I asked, and more often than not distracted me with an offering of food.

Torches lit the way as the trail curved around a dense stand of ash and birch, and opened before The Gate, a truck-sized, purplish granite boulder broken in two by real-world forces.

Dag once told me that the rock spoke of a cold, harsh world, one scoured of all life but lichens. It whispered of ice, and how the cold flow of the world carried it here only to crack and abandon it where it now stood. No magic. Only the power of glaciers.

She touched the stone and told its Ice Age story.

Sometimes Dagrun Tyrsdottir's ability to see the truth of the world frightened me more than her husband's immortal magic.

I crossed between the two halves of The Gate and into the clearing. Moonlight shimmered along The Hall's grand, golden—yet not gold—roof. The elves had imbued the earthen tiles with sun magic, and the entire building glowed.

The Hall was, in many ways, a classic Norse longhouse, with a steeply pitched roof, wood walls, and a wide central hearth. Chatter and subdued laughter poured out the open doors.

I stopped only a step beyond The Gate. The laughter, though subdued, indicated that a lot of the locals had come in this evening. Maura's melodic voice carried over the conversations. Then Axlam's sweet-sounding, semi-barked werewolf response.

Elves and werewolves. People. My shoulders tightened. My eyes blinked. I did not like crowds, even friendly, familiar crowds. Even if I came here with a purpose.

Marcus Aurelius woofed and rubbed his head against my hand.

I looked down at my hound. He looked up at me and wagged his tail. "Thank you," I said.

I heard Akeyla before I saw her. A glow of fire warmth spread out before her and the little elf I call niece burst from The Hall's entrance.

"Uncle Frank!" she sobbed, and as always, jumped into my arms. "I don't want to go back!" She hiccupped and rubbed her eyes. "I *like* Ms. Saunders."

Ms. Saunders was her third-grade teacher. "It's okay, honey." I hugged her close.

"It's *not* okay," she said. "No one will tell me why we have to go back. I like it here." She hiccupped again. "They won't let Jax come, either."

Jaxson, Gerard and Axlam's nine-year-old born-wolf son, trotted out of The Hall, dutifully following Akeyla. The Hall showed a person's true self—glamours vanished and the werewolves took wolf form—but no one's souls were stripped naked. Arne understood politics and diplomacy too well to force such a horror on all those who entered.

Jaxson, who would only be smaller than Marcus Aurelius for another year or two, sniffed my dog, sneezed and sniffled, then took up a protective stance between Akeyla and The Hall.

Nine years old and he was already showing a mate preference. Thankfully, he didn't see me as a threat. Akeyla didn't seem to notice the preference part of his friendship, or at least had yet to find fault with her friend's behavior. Still, the adults watched them carefully, just in case. As did I.

"Do you both like your teacher?" I asked as I jostled Akeyla to my hip. Perhaps I could distract them both from their sobbing.

Jaxson lifted his blue-black muzzle and yipped. Unlike both his parents, whose wolf forms could pass for the real thing, Jaxson's fur shimmered with violet-blue, icy magic. Born-wolves often "presented," as Arne liked to say, and Jaxson fully showed both his magic and his Alpha-in-the-making will.

Akeyla nodded to her friend. "Jax doesn't like Ms. Saunders." She put her head on my shoulder.

"Oh?"

She shrugged, then hugged my neck. "Are you staying for dinner?" She pouted and blinked her big eyes.

"I need to talk to your grandfather." I glanced at The Hall.

Akeyla hugged me again. "He's being mean."

Jax yipped again. He circled once, then sat again between us and The Hall entrance. His wolf magic wafted off his fur in tiny Aurora Borealis sheets. He rocked from one side to the other, and softly growled.

Jaxson Geroux was not a wolf who hid his emotions well.

Arne Odinsson strode out of his Hall. He scowled.

Out of his glamour, the full power of his magic trailed behind him as sparks in the air. Arne stood taller than most men, though a good hand shorter than me. His frame showed considerable strength, with wide shoulders and a broad chest. His hands, though, appeared elegant, if large. He watched me with deep, intense eyes the same gray as a storm, and wore the black hair crowning his head in a long, twisted, partially-braided pony-tail clasped with many bits of silver. His hair, like all the elves', waved behind his head as if alive. Thick, lynx-like sideburns grew down the sides of his face below the naked sides of his scalp.

His tall, pointed ears stood out the most. Long ago a beast had notched his left, and he wore multiple piercings in his right, to balance the effect.

The blue tattooed symbols along the sides of his head shimmered in the light radiated by The Hall. "There you two are!" Arne called. He lifted Akeyla off me and placed her on his leather-clad hip. The rest of the world might see a three-piece suit, or khakis and a sweater, but underneath, Arne Odinsson was comfortable and ready for a fight. "Are you bothering Uncle Frank? It's time to sup."

He looked more at Jaxson than his granddaughter.

The wolf-kid yipped-growled.

"Grandpa!" Akeyla yelled. She slapped his arm and wiggled until he set her on the ground. She wrapped her arms protectively around Jax's neck. "Don't yell at Jax!"

Arne spoke with a voice as flat as his face. "I have not yelled at anyone, young lady," he said.

Akeyla hiccupped again. "Come on," she said, and tugged Jax toward The Hall.

Jax's muzzle twisted downward, as did his wolf eyebrows. He yipped again, and trotted after Akeyla.

Arne tossed me a look that said *We're going to have a problem with that one.*

"Not for a decade," I said. Unless Arne did send Akeyla away.

"I know why you are here, Frank." Arne crossed his arms over his chest. "There's nothing I can do." He inhaled and continued to watch the kids as they slumped their way back into The Hall.

"Dag told me about Tyr Bragisson's call," I said. Arne did not have to agree. The elves did not clue me into their politics, but I had picked up enough to know that Arne and Dag, as a team, were at least as powerful as Dag's father. Perhaps more so.

As for the rest, I had no idea where Alfheim fell in the hierarchy of the enclaves.

"I told Maura a decade. Maybe two. Then we will bring them back with different identities." He rubbed the side of his head. "I am considering sending Gerard and Remy ahead."

He looked me directly in the eyes. "Or you."

I fully understood his unsaid order: *You've fought wars. You've protected a daughter. You understand. Take care of the Hawaiian problem.*

No, I thought. *No* not only for my own sake, but also for Akeyla's.

A raven landed in the open yard in front of The Hall's entrance. A big raven, one with pronounced throat feathers and a strong, stocky body. It hopped toward us, then to the side as it investigated the soil.

No, I thought again. I understood the pain of loneliness. I knew firsthand what happens when too much vacuum is applied to a young, raw soul. When the promise of connection—of love—is sucked away, even if that love was not real or given. The reality did not matter. Only the potential. And once it burned to death in a cottage, or lay dead on the floor of a villa, or laughed in your face, the torrential power of a cyclone stops you from breathing.

And there is no greater death-terror than asphyxiation by the willful disregard of others.

I would not enforce Arne's unspoken order. Enforcing led down a dark path, not only for me, Gerard, and Remy, but also for those for whom we enforced.

For Maura. For Akeyla.

The raven cocked its head.

Arne asked me to do this enforcing because I was ugly. Because I was a monster. Because I was an unsettled—and unstable—soul. Because I lumbered and I frightened easily-scared, tiny men.

Such enforcing came easily to my unsettled body.

"Frank?" Arne uncrossed his arms and stepped back.

My hand encircled his throat, ear to pointed ear, before either of us understood what was happening. My arm tightened.

Arne opened his mouth, but did not speak.

"I never thought I would hear you court the darker magicks, Arne Odinsson," I intoned. Murder caused cyclones and cyclones battered magic. The murder of Akeyla's father would batter hers for the rest of her life.

Long ago, murder turned me into the lumbering monster of my birth. Murder and war tore apart my soul. Murder stained *me*.

Arne clenched my wrist. He hung from my grip. His face reddened. Magic swirled in precise eddies around his hands. "Release me, Frank Victorsson."

The golden glow of The Hall's roof flickered to orange and hot red. The conversations from the interior crackled and popped. Heat grabbed ahold of my ears and my neck. Heat crawled down my spine.

Heat blackened the magic around me.

"*Frank!*" Maura screamed. She stood in The Hall's entrance with Akeyla clinging to her waist and Jax between us.

The little wolf barred his teeth and growled.

"Put me down, son," Arne said.

His hands gripped my forearm. His biceps bulged. He was strong-arming his entire weight off my wrist.

I'd picked him up by his neck and now held him in the air a good foot and a half off the ground.

I shook. How was this happening? Slowly, I lowered Arne until his feet touched the ground. "What..."

Arne rubbed his neck. "I would kill a lesser man for such an action, *jotunn*," he snarled.

His punch hit me square on the jaw. He pulled it. I knew the moment his knuckles contacted my skin.

I might bruise. I would swell for an hour or two. But Arne Odinsson decided not to dislocate, and for that, I should be grateful— yet all I wanted was to let out the fire. Let the rage dance across the surface of my life like gasoline on the lake. Let it burn where it had no business burning.

Which was wrong. Wrong in angle; wrong in line and shape. Wrong for my life and wrong for Maura and Akeyla.

Wrong for everyone.

"Arne..." I said. "Something's happening. The ghosts. Geometry..." I waved my hand at The Hall.

"Get. Out," he said. His fists clenched as if he wished to hit me again.

"Arne..."

"Get away from my Hall," he barked. "And my family."

I backed away. I had no other choice.

From The Hall's entrance, Akeyla watched. Her lip quivered. Jax leaned against her on one side, and Marcus Aurelius on the other.

Canine magic would protect my niece. Wolf and dog. *Good boys*, I thought, and lumbered for the real world.

CHAPTER 11

I parked my truck at the base of Rose's Hill. My lake was two miles behind me, and Alfheim twenty, all down a barely-visible dirt track of a road.

Dusk had settled in as I drove away from The Hall and the now-night blanketed the forest with humid, blue-black shadows. Small creatures snapped twigs. An owl hooted. Green eyes watched me from under a fallen log.

Arne would never sell off this plot of land. No noisy, intolerable neighbors would build here. Ghosts walked between these moonlit brambles.

I rubbed my face.

"What is happening?" I mumbled to myself. My dog had stayed with Akeyla. My wise, wonderful Marcus Aurelius had taken it upon himself to offer the protection I could not.

Why? Because I could not control my anger? Because it welled up still? Because I wasn't strong enough to catch it before it grasped Arne's neck?

It seemed that all the meditation in the universe could not change the base nature of an unnatural monster.

Unless....

The rage had felt as if I'd stepped across a line. Or had been pulled. And on the other side, heat lit my spine on fire.

Again with boundaries and borders. Again with veils and mixing. And fire.

I had to do something other than destroy. I had to find answers.

I dropped my boots to the cooling dirt. The path up the hill to Rose's cottage was more cut-in footholds and placed rocks than an actual walk. When she had come of age, Arne had given her the high ground, perhaps for the symbolism. Or perhaps as a daily reminder that she could choose a brave path, one different than the low, dark ways of most witches.

She'd tried. She held until the hurricanes whipped up by the Great War darkened even the magic of Alfheim.

Murder stains all magic. Rose had been particularly sensitive to discoloration. I'd been too drunk to notice until after the fact.

She'd gathered texts. Spells and enchantments. Amulets. Books and tomes and knowledge. Something might still be up there, in the ashes. A bone, perhaps. A talisman. A connection that would give me some type of insight.

Perhaps. Perhaps not. But I had to do something other than destroy.

I looked up at the hill. Could taking the notebook to the crest open its secrets? Did Rose write something on those pages that could only be seen in the presence of *her* ghost?

The landscape was dotted with puzzle pieces I could not fit together. Pieces that, honestly, looked to me to be from completely different puzzles.

But when magic was involved, there was only one puzzle. My time with Rose taught me that.

I hopped into the bed of my truck and pulled a flashlight and Rose's notebook out of my toolbox. I tied the notebook's twine to my belt, then trained the beam of my flashlight onto the scruffy birch growing along the hill's "path." I may be strong, but giants need to see to guarantee stability. Best to be prepared.

Her hill was west of the Mesabi Range—the Iron Range, the locals called it—the chain of mountain cores that buttressed Lake Superior. The Mesabi were what caused the elves to settle where they did. They'd had enough of carrying their boats over hills and through streams, and decided to stop before they hit the Central Plains of North America.

I helped build Rose's cottage at the peak of this steep hill. I helped cut in the climb to its door. I knew exactly where to look for holds among the birch, and how to get in.

I'd been a century old the last time I stepped foot inside. Now I was two, and had my life seemingly under control. I drank coffee and tea now. I meditated as best as a man such as myself could. And I made brownies with my niece.

Such were the stories I told myself.

I tapped the heel of my boot on the first set stone up to the house. It held. Rocks shifted under my boots. I tucked the flashlight into my waistband and leaned into my ascent. Shadows danced, but my unnatural eyes did well in moonlight.

But that, too, was a story. The cold, hard torch threw a beam of glare that only a mechanism of the modern world could create. I might need it, but I shouldn't, where I was going. I walked into magic … and magic, I knew, shimmered and glowed and illuminated the night well enough.

I used the birch along the side of the path as handholds. No birds chirped at me, nor did any animal scurry away. Even the plants seemed quieter than they should have been.

I emerged from the bushes and birch into the clearing in front of Rose's little house. The air changed up here—not that "up here" was more than a ten-yard climb up a steep hill. No earthen scents. No living things like the forest floor under my truck. Only rocks and faint wood ash, as if I smelled an olfactory glamour.

The enchantment Rose had set made this small patch of land more a cold, shadowed mountain valley than a real place in Minnesota. Each sharp rock shimmered black as obsidian. *Something* towered over the cottage, something not here, but enchanted to be so. The air carried an unnatural warmth and the thin, clear crispness of a wind blowing down a mountain face. The moon gleamed bluer here, as well.

But the quiet unnerved me the most. A Minnesota forest was never this quiet. Not even a mountain valley in winter was this quiet. Breezes whistled. Animals broke branches and ran tree limbs. But up here on Rose's Hill, sound became only the tactile sense of the wind.

Rose's cottage waited thirty paces across the open clearing in the gray and silver moonlight, just as tended and stable as it had been the day it was built.

It burned a century ago. It likely burned to the ground. The fire killed Rose and one of Arne's lieutenants.

I remembered very little through my stupor beyond the blinding glare and the volcanic heat. The fire had been a column to the sky. It kept everyone at bay. It kept *me* at bay. Nothing remained, so no one came up here.

There should be no house at the top of the hill.

Yet there it was, a log and slat cottage with shuttered windows and a pitched roof. The wood had weathered and blended into the dirt, as did the roof. But the door still hung on its frame, and the small, circular window in the roof's front peak still held its glass.

Was I looking at yet another ghost? "What are you?" I whispered.

The house did not answer, nor did the wind. It sat as much in silence as Lizzy and my father and their unreal geometry, except for the smoke-like halo that lunged and lurked like vipers around the cottage's foundations.

The elves felt her protection enchantment. Arne once told me it stung and pricked until the elf dropped incapacitated to the ground.

Dark, stained magic still haunted the ghost of Rose's life.

The fog lunged at my feet. I yipped and jumped like a child, but it did no good. Rose's final enchantment curled around my leg and pulled me toward the cottage.

The door wasn't right. Wood gripped my fingertips, and it appeared solid, but like everything else up here, it smelled only of wind and... ash.

Ash. Blown-in soot from a fire raging two states over. The talc of a long-extinct volcano. Pyres. Old ash, the kind that had turned to dust long ago. I peered at the grain.

The door did not simply smell of its own death, it *was* its own death. The fog—the ash—filled each edge, each valley in the wood, every splinter and every knot.

Rose's magic had made a copy of her home and when it burned, and the magic used the cinders to backfill between the lines. I stood in front of a door that was threshold-ness frozen in time and filled in with the remains of what it had once been.

How much power did she have when she died? I'd been clueless. I'd only thought she'd lost her mind. I had no idea that she'd commanded such control. I'd watched the house burn as her magic licked and burned right along with it, but I'd never figured it out.

Perhaps the elves hadn't, either.

I pushed at the door. It opened soundlessly and I stood, for the first time in a century, in the small, open, single room of Rose's life.

Books littered the floor. Papers lay strewn about. Tanned skins hung on the walls. Dried herbs—plants that long ago should have been as much dust as the ash that made this place—hung from the ceiling.

The massive walk-in hearth I'd set for her still appeared functional even in its soot-phantom form of the room around it, and her black cauldron sat on its tripod under the chimney.

It took us five years to walk the Mississippi River from Louisiana to Alfheim. I fed and clothed her along the way. Many times, I could have left her in the care of people who knew children. People who understood how to be a parent. But every night I watched her shimmer. I knew what she was. After all the death I'd inflicted during the War, I wanted to save at least one soul.

I think Arne did, as well.

It took forty years for her to explode. I was too drunk to see it coming. I'd effectively abandoned her to her isolation and her corrupted magic.

I dropped to my knees in her books and her papers. Were my

ghosts telling me to make sure the same thing didn't happen to Akeyla?

How could it? Akeyla was an elf. Her magic was pure. Unlike Rose, she wasn't a blend of human and magical.

But she was a blend of elf and spirit.

Rose had been the same age when I carried her into Arne and Dag's home and begged them to help the little witch. I claimed I knew they had the power to help her control her corrupted magic. Arne helped the werewolves. Why was helping a witch so much more difficult?

The wolves were not chaos personified. The wolves heard only their own voices and the voices of their pack. The wolves could not open doors to Hell.

Witches could. Some. Not many, to be honest, but the various provinces of The Land of the Dead were the easiest to access with magic.

The dead were always close by, as my ghosts reminded me. They lived next door. All you had to do was knock on their threshold.

And the grass is always greener on the other side, especially if you are a corrupted witch.

Which version of Hell did Rose believe in? The frozen wasteland of the Norse gods? The Abrahamic pit of fire and brimstone? Duat, the Egyptian Land of the Dead?

I untied her book from my belt and set it on the ash-floor. The wrap crinkled, and I minded the folds and lines. Best not to inadvertently release an unknown geometry while inside Rose's domain.

No words on the first page, or the second, or the third. No drawings. No lines of poetry or marks of any kind. Nothing on the cover, either. Had Rose meant to use this book, but died before she set a pen to its pages?

I picked up the book to look at its spine.

A pressed flower fell out.

A big, bright, tropical bloom of white, yellow, and red, flat and thin and the size of my hand, drifted out of the book and settled onto the wrapper below.

I'd seen flowers like this one in the bouquets sent by Akeyla's father.

Like the door, the flower was hell-soot. Symbols manifested on its petals—sharp corners with glass-like edges.

"What do you say?" I asked it.

It crumpled to dust.

I jerked back my hand. The wrapper brightened as if it was about to burst into flame, then it, too, crumpled to dust.

The book brightened, as did the ash-papers around it, and the next paper beyond it also crumpled.

And the next. And the next.

A path of hell-soot appeared before me. "Rose?" I whispered. Was she here? Was my long-dead adoptive daughter trying to tell me something?

I cautiously followed the trail toward the steps up to the cottage's sleeping loft. Did I dare take the stairs? Would they crumble like the paper?

My answer came as the trail touched the bottom step.

What had once been a wide wood loft for Rose's bed, walls of shelves, and her one, small, round window, became pinpoints of light. Some cold, some hot. The dust of ghosts became the dust of stars, and Rose's world became a portal.

Was this Rose? Akeyla's father? Or something completely different?

Either way, I knew where that portal led.

I reached out.

The protection tattoos along my scalp burst outward. Curls of force, lines of power, and interlocking mandalas of magic formed a blue, green, violet Borealis barrier between me and the stardust that had once been Rose's most private area.

I withdrew my hand. The protection spell stayed in place. Nothing from Rose's side could cross and do me harm; nor could I cross to find explanations.

Unless…

I didn't think about what I was doing. My automatic response was to mark this magic, to add a tracer so that the elves or the wolves could come back later and perhaps make sense of what was happening—or perhaps to give myself some insight. I didn't stop to consider that perhaps the protection spell was responding with a wall for a reason. It didn't occur to me that the magic I carried was, in many ways, a living thing, and that like all living things, it had automatic responses to threats that a conscious mind should not ignore.

I tossed a tracer into the protection spell's wall. Curls retracted like recoiling anemone. Mandalas rotated like gearwork inside a lock. The tracer twisted and elongated in midair, forming an arrow of magic.

I should have known better. My *body* should have known better. There was a reason I'd made it to two hundred years, and they weren't simply the resilience of my science-built chassis. I'd made it to two hundred years because I was quick on my feet.

The reality of life changed when that arrow of magic pierced whatever veil the protection spell had deemed so terrible that it needed to build a wall between it and me.

I had my answer about the hell in which Rose walked. Or no answer at all, because only the living sought knowledge.

Hel, I thought. *Duet*. Perhaps the Elysian Fields or one of the Circles of Hell. It did not matter. I'd just sent a tracer enchantment into The Land of the Dead.

I only knew the tales told about those who crossed over and somehow managed to return. I'd always suspected that each story—each myth—contained a grain of truth, but that grain wasn't what the storytellers thought it was. The stories were about the living. They were meant to teach the living lessons.

Because the dead did not seek knowledge. The dead didn't care.

The dead…

My father built me out of parts he'd stolen from the dead. He molded my flesh from clay polluted by death. Yet I walked and I sought and I obviously needed to learn a lesson.

On the other side of the protection enchantment's bright, shimmering wall of magic, on the side where an arrow of magic did its own seeking, on the side that *did not care*, something scooped up my tracer enchantment.

Ghosts were reflections of the geometry of a life's moment. Often, they repeated traumas. But like the myths of heroes who had returned from The Land of the Dead, a ghost's purpose was to educate the living.

I'd been seeing ghosts. More importantly, I'd been feeling the intrusions of the ghosts of my own rage, of my body's tensions and heat. My moment before meeting with Dag, and my unwarranted response to Arne, had been proof that I lived, even if that proof caused more harm than good.

On the other side, the tracer locked onto the mirror reflection of my proof of living. Yes, it raged, but not in a living way. It roiled like decay. It boiled with malignance. It responded only because it was driven to do so, but it did not care.

I gagged and staggered backward. Gagged and choked and wrapped my hands around my throat to protect the force that kept me alive—the blood pushed by my beating heart.

Rose understood malignance. Rose had spent decades fighting her own. She'd gone into The Land of the Dead still fighting, and even though she no longer cared, a reflection of her traumatic events still lingered on this side. Still fought and still offered a lesson to anyone capable of seeing the ghosts.

Rose had sent me Lizzy. She'd wanted me to remember that I could grow and change. That I was alive.

She'd sent me the ghost of my father to remind me that I was also dead.

I stumbled. My feet betrayed me and I crashed into the magic holding the dust of her cottage's door inside its ghost.

My protection enchantment's wall popped like a bubble.

The vision of the volcanic mountainside vanished. The cottage ruptured and also vanished. I lay face up on top of a leaf-strewn Minnesota forest floor, still gagging, staring at a wavering moon about to burst into fullness.

The only reality left at the top of Rose's Hill was my heaving body.

I knew what was happening. I understood what had crawled below Alfheim's magic under the cover of night.

A raven cawed. Something scurried next to my head. A bark echoed through the trees.

"Marcus Aurelius?" I coughed just as the blackness took my consciousness.

CHAPTER 12

Many types of werewolves walk the Earth. The Americas had
their own flavor of wolf who tended to be bigger and tamer
than their Old World forebears, and hewed closer to the popular
Hollywood mythology. The Geroux brothers were old French
Catholic *loup-garou*, and two of the other wolves in the pack were
descended from the beasts of the Scottish moors. Axlam, though
changed by another *loup-garou*, presented her own unique version at
each full moon.

The elves had their own version of diversity that mirrored the
cultures of the world.

In fact, the magical creatures of the world were as widely varied as
the mundanes. I'd forgotten just how widely varied.

Most of them did not have the knowledge or the inclination to
cross borders or pierce veils. Most of them didn't understand magic
beyond their own personal flavors.

But every so often, someone got angry enough to motivate
inquiries and attempts. Someone opened doors they should not. And
when those doors opened, things took advantage.

Dark, angry, dead things motivated by hungers more than by any
need to live.

Things which, even though they reside in the dankest parts of each and every version of Hell out there, carry enough maleficence to manifest a version of caring.

Someone slapped my cheek. "Frank?" a male voice said. Then a puff filled my mouth.

I still couldn't see. I'd lost consciousness. I'd dropped over like a sack of potatoes because I'd been an idiot and sent a tracer enchantment into the jaws of Hell itself.

Another puff forced its way into my throat.

"Frank!" The man slapped me again.

Somewhere in the distance, a dog barked. I gasped. Air slid into my lungs, but the world stayed black.

Someone pried open one of my eyelids and flashed a light at my pupil.

I slapped away the hand. "I'm awake!" I shook my head hoping to drive off all the afterimage circles and dots.

Ed Martinez sat back on his heels. "You weren't breathing."

I attempted to sit up. It didn't work. I fell flat on my back again.

"Why the hell are you up here?" Ed asked. He waved his hand at the flat meadow that had long ago replaced the burned-out husk of Rose's cottage.

Without the enchantments, only the hearth remained. Under the silver moonlight, the big granite boulders that made up the chimney shimmered as if they'd caught the world in their internal quartz flecks.

I'd set those stones with the same precision and care as I'd given Lizzy's cairn.

"What is this place?" Ed asked.

I forced myself onto my hands and knees. "How did you get up here?"

Ed pocketed his flashlight. "I climbed, same as you." He nodded toward the trail. "I knew something went down at that old hotel the elves like to use. I could tell when you came stumbling out like a drunk."

He frowned like a father who'd just caught his son with his first

77

sneaked beer. "Then your dog showed up with Arne right behind him." He sniffed and looked away. "Damn angry elf, that one."

"Arne's never taken you inside?" Ed was town sheriff. He knew about the magicals. Why hadn't Arne granted him at least the courtesy of knowing what "that old hotel" really was?

But I knew. There were rules.

There were always rules, with the elves.

"No..." Ed clearly understood that the hotel was someplace special. He just didn't know why.

I rubbed at my neck. The constriction in my throat continued, and my muscles still pulsed with my heartbeat.

I was alive. "Where's my dog? He was supposed to stay with Akeyla." The barking had to be Marcus Aurelius.

Ed stood. "Well, he didn't. He's down by your truck." He dusted off his knees. "Honestly, I wouldn't have found you without his insistent yelping."

I'd remembered something about wolves and magical creatures and diversity. About the dead and the living and ghosts. And I'd learned a lesson.

I checked my forearm. All but one of my tracer enchantments marched up my skin with shimmering, magical precision. I glanced around the Hill. No magic anywhere. None. Nothing on the lone hearth or clinging to the meadow grasses. No shimmers beyond the moonlight. No scent of cold mountain air, or soot, or ghosts.

Just me, Ed, and my barking dog down below.

But that didn't mean there wasn't still magic here. Magic about which Rose wanted me to know. I shook my head, trying to remember what I'd learned.

"I think Maura's ex enchanted a flower," I said. "I think it got by the elves. He wanted to open a portal." *Idiot*, I thought. "I don't think he managed."

I think *something else* managed.

"My anger, the ghosts, maybe even what happened at the café—I think it all might have been warnings." Harbingers. Calls from the other side. They were connected somehow, even if I wasn't quite sure how.

"Warnings?" Ed asked.

I inhaled deeply and tried to settle my unsettled body. "I see magic," I said. "The elves' magic appears as sheets of Aurora Borealis light. The wolves' magic is similar. But not all magic from all sources will look the same."

Ed *humphed.*

I might perceive Hawaiian magic differently—or not at all. But that didn't mean it wouldn't affect me, or Alfheim.

Or light up the route Maura's ex tried to use to make his portal.

"This might be a lot worse than an attempted visitation by a creepily persistent ex," I said. "Do you know the land easiest to bridge? The one closest to the surface? The realm easiest to access with magic?"

Ed took off his hat and ran his hand over the top of his head. "The place where ghosts and demons come from?"

I nodded. "The Land of the Dead." The place the magic left behind by Rose was keen on me noticing.

Ed placed his hat back on his head. "Which one?"

"They're all different locations in the same territory," I said.

He sniffed. "Of course they are." He shook his head. "And Maura's ex thought he could walk through for a visit?"

I pointed at the hearth. "Except he's fire magic. Too chaotic. I don't think he knew what he was doing."

Ed rubbed his face. "He's just belligerent enough to think the consequences didn't matter as long as he got to talk to his woman." He shook his head. "Why are these asses so damned predictable?"

I feared the worst of the dead had used Maura's ex's belligerence as an escape route.

"We need to find the point of enchantment." I pointed at the path. "I think a hitchhiker came through."

Something from The Land of the Dead with enough motivation to overcome the lack of caring that was death. Something strong and cunning. Something smart enough to notice a portal, and to use it.

Ed grunted and looked up at the sky. "Of *course* something else came through. Isn't that the price of admission with magic? Bad crawling out of the dungeon?"

I rose up on my knees. "Where's the book?" Rose used that book to show me the truth. Maybe it would tell me how to kill the hitchhiker.

I glanced around. No wrapped package anywhere. No unwrapped ones, either.

"What book?" Ed waved his flashlight.

"Ivan gave me one of Rose's notebooks," I said. "I brought it with me. Thought maybe I could read it in Rose's space. Gather some insight."

Ed trained his flashlight on my chest. "You got a *magic notebook* from a *vampire* and you brought it into the domain of a dead *witch*?" He sounded as if he wanted to slap the living daylights out of me. "And you're wondering why something *nasty* hijacked a dumbass's attempt to harass his ex? Now who's bullheaded about the consequences of magic?"

He had a point. "I didn't realize what was happening until I opened the book in there," I pointed at the hearth, "and an enchanted tropical flower fell out."

Ed frowned.

"It worked, didn't it?" I rubbed at my neck again. "Rose showed me the truth."

Ed did not respond, but his face said *Sure thing, buddy.*

"The book was blank." I rubbed at my neck yet again. "No obvious spells." And again. "I don't think it's actually blank."

Not if a flower fell out of it.

"Of course it's not blank!" Ed yelled. "Nothing a witch touches is ever *blank*."

Ed swung his flashlight around again. "You got that notebook from those two creepy shits? The Bitersons? Why the hell does Arne let them stay in Alfheim? They're *vampires*. They're *dangerous*."

And yet Ed stayed in Alfheim, too. "The same reason he brought you in, Ed," I said. "Same as me. Arne likes to care for wayward souls."

Ed's guffaw turned into a choked snort. "You know damned well why I brought my family here." He brushed off his thigh. "After I killed that vamp, the clans took it personally." He waved his arms at the wider world. "Do you think my kids like the snow? Do you think I enjoy the blizzards? Minnesota ain't nearly as nice as you people like to think it is. But that's okay. Vampires *won't get us here*."

Every single hair on the back of my neck stood on end. Every one of my scars tingled. My stomach crunched in on itself and it wasn't from the magical ordeal I'd just survived. No, this feeling was here-and-now.

"Ed," I said as I pushed myself to my reluctant feet, "My head's mushy." So much swirled.

He didn't move to help support my weight. I towered over him and outweighed him by a good hundred-plus pounds. No use in him getting hurt if I stumbled into him.

Ed's demeanor stiffened. "Because of the same reason you stumbled out of the hotel? Or because of other reasons?" He stopped playing dad and turned one hundred percent cop. He looked around and his hand landed on his service weapon.

Ed, it seemed, was having the same subconscious fear and alert responses as I was.

"Both, I suspect," I said.

He moved toward me, his hand still on his weapon, and turned so we were back-to-back. "I followed you from the Mayor's office," he said. "I figured she'd send you to talk to Maura."

"She did."

Ed nodded. "I wanted to ask her some questions."

"I know that, Ed." The shadows around the hearth slipped. They shuddered a miniscule, tiny bit, a usually unnoticeable amount, but I had the dead caring enough to try to teach me a lesson.

"Do you know much about how vampires enthrall their victims?" Ed asked.

There were as many types of vampires as there were werewolves. Maybe more. The world—and Americans in particular—seemed to be enamored with taming the horror that was the murderous bloodsucker. Since the end of World War II, vampires had become the dapper, charismatic stand-in for all the bad things mundanes did to each other.

But evil was evil no matter how handsome and charming it presented itself to be. No matter how it manipulated and, as Maura described it, "gaslit." Seemed her ex liked to lie and reframe events to make himself out as the victim.

Maura called it gaslighting. I called it pathetic, sniveling, conniving, worm behavior. And pathetic, sniveling, conniving, worm behavior was exactly how vampires acted.

"I know, Ed," I said. But unlike an abusive mundane, vampires had malignant magic to make their gaslighting all that much easier.

"See, Frank, shit like what went down at the café went down in a couple of the towns in my county back in Texas. Weird, odd, stuff that messed over some young woman. It happened for about three, maybe five years. Everyone thought it was par for the course, you know? Young men can be terrible human beings."

So many mundanes can be terrible human beings. Even the good people of Alfheim closed ranks and refused to help outsiders in need.

"Then it escalated. The women started vanishing. I started finding parts."

I knew some of the story. The vampire had taken at least ten women and four men.

"I had never in my life been so thankful as the day I learned that the world really did have magical creatures."

Arne and the Geroux brothers had learned about the killings and traveled to the site to investigate, thinking that they had a rogue were-wolf on their hands.

Not a wolf. A vampire.

Very few demons were motivated, cunning, and perceptive. But certain motivations will wind up a demon. Certain motivations will call it back to where it could feed.

"Something about the café raised my hackles," Ed said. "And it wasn't just your ghosts, Mr. Victorsson. The speed at which those two uploaded the video. The fact that they knew who and when to film.

The weird effects not only on little Akeyla, but also on you." He unclipped his weapon. "I had a feeling."

Marcus Aurelius stopped howling.

The shadows by the hearth twitched.

"The hitchhiker is a vampire, isn't it?" Ed asked.

Primordial hunger and addiction could motivate a demon.

A *vampire* had come through, and not an everyday bloodsucker like Tony or Ivan. This was one of the demon-like shades, the anti-life thing that possesses a human and turns him or her into vampire.

This one felt like a vampire god.

I pushed him toward the path. "Go!" I said.

Ed ran. I yanked my big torch light off its loop on my belt and swung it first toward the route down, so Ed had some idea of where to go.

Then I swung it back at the shadows.

Blackness punched me in the face.

CHAPTER 13

A right jab hit me square in the nose. My septum moved, but thankfully did not snap. My head jerked; my shoulders followed. I dropped the flashlight as I rotated, but kept enough of my wits to duck as the shadow swung again.

Whatever hit me was more than seven feet tall, strong—and cloaked in ash-filled shadows. Mist swirled around it like black silk death-shrouds.

It danced out of the light's beam.

Why hadn't my protection enchantments kicked on the way they had inside the ghost-cottage? Their purpose was to protect me from the intentional harm inflicted by magic—elven, fae, witch, white, black, vampire, or anything in between. Yet, like my tracers with Lizzy, not one of my tattoos responded.

The creature landed a kick to my left kidney.

I understood pain. I had awakened into life full of pain so sharp, so cutting, so utterly raw that it pulsed along my flesh. I used to live inside that shell of anguish, of sensitivity to the noises of the world, to the chirping of birds. To the scents of cooking. To animals.

The new pain radiating outward from my lower back was all my previous torment distilled down to one knife-like wound.

I bellowed and buckled over. The creature laughed. Then a blinding, white light exploded in front of my eyes.

Ed trained his flashlight—and his gun—on my head. "Stand down!" he yelled.

Not on my head. On the shadows behind my head. Stars popped in my vision, and a tunnel formed.

I couldn't pass out. I couldn't leave Ed alone with whatever had walked through an abuser's portal.

The thing danced out of the light, but Ed's beam didn't follow. I looked up at his face.

He couldn't see it. His eyes weren't tracking the wisps of shadows it left behind.

"Turn the light on yourself!" I bellowed. It didn't like the light. Maybe it would leave Ed alone if he was bathed in it.

"But…"

The thing lunged past me.

"Now!" I yelled.

Ed turned the flashlight toward his face and immediately shouted a loud, long stream of Latin church words.

The creature pulled up short. Small tendrils of smoke-like shadow poked toward Ed's face, pulled back, then wrapped around his legs.

I snatched my flashlight off the grass and illuminated Ed's entire front. My hand wavered as I swallowed down the need to vomit up my kidney, but I would not allow this thing to harm a good man with a good family.

Ed shouted another string of holy words. A laugh I couldn't pinpoint echoed through the meadow. Latin only worked on a subset of Old World vampires and other dark creatures, which this one obviously was not.

Ed switched to Spanish. Again, the thing laughed. Ed tried French, then what I guessed to be Mandarin.

The creature laughed and swirled around the meadow's shadows as if Ed's preparedness was the funniest thing it had ever encountered in its malevolent life.

Whatever kind of primordial vampire it was, it didn't believe we could do it harm, and from its lack of response to Ed's holy words, it was probably correct.

I pulled myself up and slowly moved toward Ed. "Keep the light on you," I said. Just as slowly, with my arm held tight against my side because of my kidney, I dropped a tracer enchantment into my fist.

Would it work? I doubted it would make a difference. But I had to try.

"We know what you are," I said. "You've lost your power of surprise." Vampires, like most predators, left an area once they could no longer stalk their pray. And a running vampire was easier to track and kill.

It laughed again. "Are you sure?"

"Sure enough," I said.

The shadows spun. Wisps became streamers and curls become coils, and for a moment, it took on a human shape. "It's a new world, son of Victor, with new ways of living."

The smoke hardened. It folded and it molded and the thing stared at me out of obsidian eyes. "And so many paths to death."

I whipped a tracer enchantment at a mannequin made of shadows.

Nothing flickered. No trails of smoke or lights, but the energy in the air changed. The air freshened and the light cleared. The meadow's grass came into focus. Night sounds returned.

The vampire vanished—but not my tracer.

"Damn it!" I yelled. "It shook the tracer enchantment." We wouldn't be able to locate it again. Not easily.

"Is it gone?" Ed mumbled. "The vamp in Texas couldn't alter what we saw to that extent. It couldn't inflict like…"

He vomited onto the grass.

I staggered over. My demi-health made me cold, scarred, corpselike, but it also meant my body did not deviate from its normal systemic state. And right now, that meant fixing its damaged kidney much faster than if I'd been born human.

It hadn't touched Ed other than encircling his legs. Was he bitten? Did it drain life force? Some vampires—and some witches—had mastered draining life without leaving a mark on their victims.

I checked the back of his neck for bites. "You okay? Are you bleeding? Did it bite you?" Some vampires could also bite and then heal the wound. "Do you feel dizzy?" Ed did look ashen.

"I don't think it bit me." He wiped his mouth with the back of his hand. "You?"

"My nose hurts." I rubbed the bridge. "The kidney is healing. I don't think vampires like my blood." I'd yet to have one try to bite me. Punch and attack, yes. But bite, no.

"We need to call this in," Ed said. "Arne needs to know. So do Gerard and Remy." He rubbed his shoulder. "I…" He looked up at the moon. "You know how people ignore tales of ghosts? How they say that poltergeists are all in the victim's head?"

I nodded. "Usually, they are."

Ed shook out his arm. "That's what I thought… felt… I don't know, while it was here. I *knew* you were reacting to something. I *knew* it was here, but I couldn't see or hear it." He sighed. "I couldn't sense it at all. Nothing. Yet I *knew*."

Perhaps Ed also had a sensitivity to magic. Not visually, like me, but perhaps in some subconscious way.

"What the hell do I tell my deputies?" he asked.

"I don't know." The last time I'd dealt with a vampire was in the sixties. It had been preying on students on my college campus. It paid for feedings, though. Everybody knew about the sugar daddy with the weird sexual tastes.

That vampire hadn't been… smoky. I glanced back at the hearth. The house had been here. Rose's *life* had been here. But it had been ash.

The damned thing had cloaked itself in a witch's ashes.

I helped Ed toward the path. "What did you tell them last time? In Texas?"

Ed stared at the moon. "That we had a vicious serial killer." He shook as if a ghost was drawing its finger up his spine. "I don't think it's that simple this time."

This one hadn't yet killed, and part of me wondered if it would.

This one was different. The ash-shadow veil, the laughter, the hiding on a witch's property. The messing with the lives of elves.

Maybe we weren't dealing with a vampire-demon. Maybe we were dealing with something worse.

I pointed my flashlight at the path. "We need to talk to—" I realized I hadn't heard Marcus Aurelius since before the creature attacked.

"My dog!" I said, and ran for the path.

CHAPTER 14

The emperor was nowhere to be found. He wasn't in the back of my truck, or waiting next to Ed's cruiser. He didn't come when I called.

"Look." Ed pointed at the dirt track that served as the road. "Tracks."

Marcus Aurelius had run away from the vehicles and back toward the lake. After about fifty yards, his tracks veered into the woods where I lost them in the gloom.

"Here, boy!" I called. Perhaps he'd hidden because of the vampire creature.

No rustling. No yipping, no padding of dog feet.

"We'll come back in the morning," Ed said. "I want another look at the site."

I had no other option. Tracking a dog into a dark forest in the middle of the night wasn't a good idea even without malevolence on the prowl.

Ed patted my arm. "That thing was on top of the hill with us. It couldn't have gotten him." He pointed at the trees. "He's hiding. He's smart. We'll get him in the morning."

What if Ed was wrong and I'd let down not only Akeyla, but also my dog? I closed my eyes and pressed my fingers into my forehead. I didn't have the option of such thinking. Not while a vampire stalked Alfheim.

I pulled out my phone and dialed. No answer from Arne. He must still be at The Great Hall. "We found the real problem," I said to his voice mail, and hung up.

Dag answered her phone. She sniffed as if she could smell black magic on me from the other side of the connection. "I take it you found something at Rose's Hill?"

"Yes."

"I'll come to your place." She hung up.

I stared at my phone for a long moment. "That was odd."

Ed chuckled. "Odd? After what we just survived?"

I tucked my phone into my pocket. "Call the Geroux brothers. Tell them what happened. Then take your wife and kids to stay with the wolves."

Ed looked back at the hill. He frowned, and the two of us stood silent in the forest, still a good fifty yards down the track from our vehicles. I almost asked him to turn off his flashlight. I almost turned off mine. I almost asked him to breathe in the rich, earthy, night magic of the land. To let it cleanse away the malevolent smoke we'd both breathed at the top of the hill.

But I didn't. Inviting in shadows right now was too dangerous.

Ed adjusted his belt. He'd left his weapon unsnapped, just in case.

Yes, it was most definitely too dangerous to walk in the dark right now.

"Yeah," he said. "I think you are a wise man, Mr. Victorsson."

I PULLED the truck up to my garage. Dag's roadster sat off to the side, under the motion-sensing string of lights between my house and the side gate. The lights give the area a nice, warm glow, and I've found that the few visitors I get prefer them to a massive halogen bursting on as they drive up.

Dag's roadster is as sleek and powerful as its owner. It's also the same shade of gray-blue-green as her magic.

She'd been surprised when I told her that, but it made her smile.

The elves, for all their bluster and power, were just as much people as the mundanes of the town. Maybe more so, in some cases. The long-lived elves had an understanding of life that the younger ones did not.

Dag had that understanding, a sort of perfecting of the act of living. She, like Arne and a few of the other powerful elves, had lived multiple lifetimes. Not just multiple centuries, but multiple identities with multiple families.

Maura was not Dag and Arne's only child. She was just their only modern one.

And, I suspected, the most free of all their children. Free, because she lived in a time when her father would not marry her off for political gain.

Dag understood. Dag treasured. Dag did not want her daughter to return to a situation where she lost her freedom.

My gate, with its iron scrollwork and its drilled, colorful, repurposed wine bottles, was an overly-artsy gift from Maura. She'd commissioned it while she still lived in Hawaii and had it delivered out of the blue one day. I'd never asked why, and didn't plan to. The gate was lovely, a work of art created by one of the many artists who lived nearby, even if it was odd. I installed it immediately, and display it proudly.

It stood open.

Dag waited on my deck, her back to the house and her magic a shimmering, swirling plume around her otherwise glamoured body.

From behind, she looked appropriately middle-aged to be Maura's mother. Fifty-ish, perhaps—still young enough to have another child if she wanted, which gave her an air of fertility goddess. Good "mayor" age, she liked to say. Good for culling subconscious respect from the mundanes.

But tonight, she looked small and crushed inward, as if the weight of her centuries had finally settled onto her shoulders.

She inhaled as I rounded the corner of the house. Her plume of magic responded by shrinking in on itself in small bursts that seemed to mimic her beating heart.

I think it noticed me before she did.

Her glamour shifted and that sense of the weight of years—of life —vanished. Dagrun Tyrsdottir became, once again, the elf no one dared annoy.

"Frank," she said, as she pointed at the glass and chrome monstrosity across the lake. "I had no idea they were going to build *that*." Her sniff settled into a frown. "It's Danish modern, at least."

I chuckled. "Danish glass and chrome reflect just as much unwanted glare through my windows as any other culture's modern nonsense."

Dag smiled, but it quickly vanished. "Maura and Akeyla will not leave The Great Hall until I say so."

I had expected as much, but the way Dag said it made me wonder. "You overruled Arne, didn't you?"

Her eyes narrowed. "He should not have run you out of The Hall. He should have gone with you to Rose's Hill." She turned her back to me again. "Do not expect an apology or any acknowledgement of his mistake."

Their argument must have been intense for her to say such a thing. But it wasn't the emotional or even the social awkwardness that clenched up my gut. Her words were a coded "Do not expect help from Arne."

He would help, but he would not be helpful, because he was mad at me for showing disrespect, even though no disrespect was meant.

I closed my eyes and did my best not to sigh.

Dag clicked her tongue. When I opened my eyes again, she wore an expression that clearly indicated how well we understood each other.

Arne had likely locked onto sending Maura back to Hawaii to show his kingdom how well he had the situation under control.

Dag chuckled. "I'm the one married to him."

"Maura and Akeyla," I pointed at my house. "They can't go back."

Her grip on her elbows tightened. "I know. Arne says he'll send you or Remy or one of the other wolves to be her guard dog for the decade she has to live on that island." She looked back at the lake. "He's been King so long he no longer understands how intimate terror works."

She rubbed her forehead and changed the subject. "Tell me what happened at Rose's Hill."

"Ed's fetching his family. I told him to go to the wolves until we deal with this thing."

Dag inhaled. "What did you find?"

"It felt like the evil that replaces a person's soul, when they turn." I shook my head. Every vampire was a dual soul. All vampires were possessed. "A vampire-demon. I think Maura's ex inadvertently gave it access to Alfheim. I think that idiot thought he could make a portal through The Land of the Dead."

"And this vampire-demon noticed the path," Dag said.

I nodded.

"Do you think one of the clans is taking advantage to send an assassin north for Ed?" Her face hardened. "I will personally kill every vampire on this continent if any harm comes to the Martinez family." She inhaled again. "I will kill them all if they caused the harm that has befallen my daughter."

The plume of magic around Dag erupted into a bright tornado of white, blue, and green aurora sheets. It spun for a long moment, then twisted down into what looked like magical armor.

Never, in my two centuries with the elves, had I ever seen any of their magic manifest the way it was manifesting around Dag right now.

"Tell me what you see, Frank Victorsson," she whispered.

"Your magic." I traced the outline of a sigil manifesting over her shoulder. "It's building around you like a suit of armor."

Her nod was almost imperceptible. "If ever there was proof of your ability to see magic, it is this moment, son of Victor." She held up her hand before I could answer. "Tell me of the creature."

"It hits hard." I brushed my hand over my kidney. "I could see it. Ed

93

could not." Now I inhaled. "It did not have magic I recognize. Not the way you do, or Rose did. It cloaked itself in death and ash."

"And you are sure it was a vampire?"

"Honestly, I don't know. Ed's instincts say vampire, as do mine. But, as I said, it was cloaked." I shook my head. "Though I do think it is a demon."

She nodded.

"There's something else." How was I to explain? "I stopped at the library earlier today."

Dag turned her body fully toward mine and dropped her hands off her elbows. "Continue."

"I wanted to see if there was anything in Rose's papers about ghosts." There was a bouquet on the counter at the library. One with huge tropical blossoms.

How stupid could I have been? Damned vampires. They were as sneaky as they were evil. "Ivan gave me a notebook. It was blank. Looked blank. I took it with me to Rose's Hill to see if being in her space made whatever she recorded visible."

The truth was I didn't know whether Ivan or Tony called the creature, or if it was attracted to them because their proximity to the flowers, or even if it was a vampire.

"The creature has the book?" Dag did not, at all, look surprised. If anything, she looked like a mother waiting for a child to explain for himself his misdeeds.

I tapped my head. "It vanished before the creature showed up, so I don't know if he took it or not." *Rose could have taken it*, I thought, but did not say.

Dag walked over. She leaned her head to the side and looked up at my face. "What is the common thread here?"

I shook my head. "Boundary crossing. Veil piercing. Disguises."

Dag tapped my chest. "The approaching Samhain makes those magicks easier to wield. That is all. They are tools."

Tools to expose my personal weaknesses? I frowned. Why would a vampire target me?

She patted my chest. "I believe Ivan needs a visit."

No one other than Arne visited the Bitersons at night. No one was that stupid. "In the morning?" I asked. "I left Marcus Aurelius in the woods. Ed thinks he's hiding. If the—"

Her fingers curled and she pressed the tips into my flesh. "Come."

With that, the Queen of Alfheim, an elf cloaked in armor-magic, walked toward her roadster.

CHAPTER 15

The windows of the Ramsey Mansion Library glowed as if Hell itself had set the interior on fire. Thankfully, we were well past closing time, and no mundanes were around. Very few drove by on the highway, and I suspected that those who did would not see anything unusual.

The glow was purely magic.

I pointed. "That cannot be good."

Dag hoisted her quiver onto her back. The arrows glimmered in the moonlight, each enchanted with elven magic. She pulled one out and held it out for me to see.

Only the very tip of the arrow glinted with metal. The rest of the arrowhead and the shaft had been fashioned out of the one continuous sapling branch.

"Oak," Dag said. "Best for vampires. The tip is silver." She placed the arrow back into her quiver.

Dag touched my arm. "Tony and Ivan have lived among us for decades."

I knew exactly what she meant—this was not a clear-cut, black and white situation. Ivan might have meant to trick me, or he might have been tricked himself by the magic of the book. Or everyone might be lying. Or not. I was not to break anyone's head until we had answers.

I nodded and took point. Vampires did not like my blood, but a few of them had a taste for elf. Tony and Ivan, supposedly did not, but the creature might be a different story.

And from the unnatural glow coming from the windows, we could be walking into anything, including the creature lounging on top of the library desk reading one of Tony's bodice-rippers.

The library's doors blew open. Tony flew over the threshold.

He bounced down the steps—bones cracking and lungs gasping for air—and landed at my feet.

Vampires are tough. Landing the way he did on the last three steps would have killed a mundane man. Tony groaned, snapped his shoulder back into its socket, and licked the blood off his lip.

He stayed on his back on the granite between the topiaries, obviously in too much pain to move. "Mr. Victorsson. Mayor Tyrsdottir," he said. "I'm humbled our King felt the need to call in reinforcements."

Dag looked down at Tony, then up at the door. "Arne!" she yelled.

Bright, blinding white magic erupted through the open door. I cringed and squinted, and reflexively shielded my eyes.

Tony wiped blood off the corner of his mouth as he watched. "Fascinating," he intoned.

Arne's lynx bounded out the door. He growled and flicked his stubby tail, then sat down and began licking his paw and cleaning his fluffy, tipped ear.

"Gaupe?" Dag walked up the steps toward the cat. "Why are you here?"

The lynx ignored her and continued to clean his face.

Tony snickered. "Your husband's got a genuine mad-on, Mayor Tyrsdottir." He slowly pushed himself to sitting. "I'm surprised he didn't bring his canine helpers."

"Arne!" Dag yelled again. She pulled an arrow and armed her bow before returning to the landing and kicking Tony's thigh. "Speak!"

He held up his hands. "Seems the sheriff called our King and told him his daughter let in a rogue vampire." He sniffed. "I *told* him that neither Ivan nor I sensed another vampire! Do you think I want some crazy bastard in our territory? How will that help me? I have a good thing going here."

Dag lowered her bow.

Tony thrust out his chin. "Vampires cannot stay in one life. We cannot build." He rubbed at his belly. "Unless we align ourselves with one of the clans. Who wants that? You two have no idea. The world's prima donna vampires control the planet's strategic reserves of back-stabbing bitchiness."

Dag rolled her eyes. "Perhaps I should put you out of your misery, Mr. Biterson."

Tony's lip curled and for a split second, a fang showed.

But he pulled it back and grinned. "Why Mayor Tyrsdottir, I do believe your compassion is showing."

Faster than I could draw breath, Dag drew her bow. Tony snickered.

"Tony…" When he looked up at me, I shook my head.

Tony sighed and slowly stood. "I apologize, my beautiful Elf Queen of the Upper Midwest." He winked. "You betcha."

Dag poked Tony in the chest with the tip of her arrow. "Speak of my husband."

Tony wisped his hand through the air like an Eighteenth-Century fop. "Our handsome Elf King broke my locks." He pointed at the wide-open door. "That's gonna cost, ya know."

Dag poked him again.

"Yes, yes. He seems to believe we have some control over all things vampiric." Tony brushed the front of his t-shirt. "He's not using his inside voice. Scared the living daylights out of poor Ivan."

Tony wisped his hand again. "My dear brother took off. I should have followed the moment our King started frothing at the mouth but no, I had to do the honorable thing and protect the books."

"You only protect yourself, vampire," Dag said. She poked Tony again.

"Dag," I said. "We don't know what we're up against. This is not the way to deal with this situation."

Slowly, Tony popped and realigned his spine. He made a great show of holding his lower back. "Mr. Victorsson gets it. I tried to tell Lord Odinsson! But alas, he does not wish to listen."

Dag looked at the door.

Tony leaned toward me. "Our King has taken a 'kill them all and let the gods of the dead sort them out' attitude with us less desirables." He frowned. "Nice to know what we truly mean to the community."

"Tony. Not now," I said.

He threw out his arms. "Oh, who's he going to take his ire out upon? You, Mr. Victorsson?" He rolled his eyes. "They like their pet *jotunn*."

Dag ran up the stairs.

I wagged my finger at Tony. "Do not run off." Tony would be gone when I came out. Ivan, it seemed, already was gone. Neither vampire wanted to be anywhere near an angry elf in the midst of... what? A fight? A tantrum? Both?

"Sure thing, Mr. Victorsson, sir!" He snarled. "It is not wise, what the Elf King does," he hissed.

A new, bright, blinding flash of magic burst from every open window and door, from under shutters and through cracks in the mortar. From under the foundation and through the ground itself.

The Ramsey Mansion lifted off its moorings. The *world* lifted off its moorings.

Dag ran into the library. I ran after her, and rounded the corner into the library's antechamber.

The inlaid lines on the floor, the ones denoting the seasons and their midpoints, hovered over the granite. The entire inch-thick surface of the stone had uncoupled from the rest of the floor and now floated at least six inches in the air.

Dag put out her arm to stop me from getting too close. "My husband will not be himself," she said.

Arne's magic had bleached the interior of the library. The children's play area now appeared as if built from the muted, sparkly colors of an opal. The carvings over the main desk had turned bone white. Every book was now a washed-out, pale version of its former self.

No, Arne would not be himself after unleashing that much magic.

"Is your creature here, Mr. Victorsson?" Dag asked.

I stepped over the raised season lines and into the library proper, and scanned for shadows. "No," I said. "Whatever Arne's doing has filled the building with an even magical brightness. There's no place for it to hide."

Dag lowered her bow. "Yes," she said. "Thank you."

She also stepped over the lines and into the library. Gently, she picked up a book off one display table, flipped through it, and set it back down. "The enchantment has been evenly applied to all surfaces." She touched the counter of Tony's librarian desk. "No undulations or vibrations in areas usually thick with vampire viscosity."

She stopped in front of an empty vase.

The flowers that were there this morning when Ivan gave me the book were gone. Not coated in magic like every other surface in the library, but physically taken away. "Sam sent a bouquet not too long ago." I pointed at the vase. "The flowers looked fresh when I was here earlier today."

Dag nodded.

The library shook, and just as it had when we were outside on the steps, it lifted off its worldly moorings.

The bleaching increased. Every book, every tabletop and toy turned white. Every wall, every carving, even the ravens among the play-branches over the children's play area.

Dag stiffened. She swooped her fingers through the air in a criss-cross pattern, then drew a circle.

A gearwork-looking sigil formed between her and the vase. The gears clicked forward with what felt to me to be each beat of Dag's heart. The room filled with her beat, with her magic and power, and she closed her eyes.

Dag placed her hand in the middle of the sigil. The gears stopped. Dag gasped.

The sigil vanished. In its place, an image of Arne setting fire to the flowers that had once filled the vase.

Dag withdrew her hand. "He's systematically destroying all possible portals from The Land of the Dead." She nodded toward the door. "How do I explain to Sam why her entire inventory vanished overnight? Arne will not allow her to restock until this is finished." Dag slapped the counter.

"Why is the library—"

Another shock ricocheted through the building.

Dag held up her hand. "My husband is eradicating *every* portal, Frank. That includes every item Rose ever touched, and..." She clamped her lips closed.

"And what, Dag?"

He would go after the ghosts, as well. My ghosts. Which meant all vestiges of Lizzy left on this Earth.

"I'll kill him first," I said. I would snap the neck of the man I thought of as my father if he dared to take from me my memories.

"Frank..." Dag was looking at my eyes. "Your neck is tensing."

My hand had her by the throat as if it moved on its own. As if the bits and pieces of me that made my arm were once again a part of someone else.

Dag's magic solidified under my hand. Heat stung my palm. Her magic expanded.

I couldn't hold on. Her armor forced my grip off her neck.

But she didn't hit me the way Arne had at The Great Hall. She touched my arm, then my face, then my chest. "Frank, this is not right."

I looked down. In the bleached magic of Arne Odinsson's rage, I... glowed. Not glowed—it was more like a mirage of my body's lives lifted off my skin.

They were mostly integrated, my parts. But a patch here, another there, did not quite line up. I was a patchwork man, a haphazard pile of bone and sinew, and my life force showed it.

Arne Odinsson burst through the door from the basement. The door slammed against the wall with an ear-splitting, metallic *snap*.

The bleaching effect popped like a balloon. The library instantly returned to its normal, unmagical self. My sense of my own dislocation vanished right along with Arne's magic.

"You were supposed to cleanse any traces of that scum from all the flowers, woman," Arne yelled. "I will go to that island and I will flay that bastard's skin from his fire spirit body!"

Dag raised her bow. And Dag, in less than a blink of her eye, fired an arrow at her husband's head.

He caught it, spun his arm over his head, and behind his back. In one beautiful, dance-like movement, he transferred the arrow—and its momentum—to his other hand.

He threw it at me.

I was not a vampire. It would not kill me, but it would hurt. I twisted out of its way, sliding to the side as it collided with the space I had occupied.

It hit my bicep. All that had been white turned blazing hot and red. All that had been me became a collection of holes in which what should have been integrated was now separate.

My hand—the one that had grabbed Dag by the throat—grabbed the arrow and yanked.

I bellowed. Blood dripped from the wound. Dag looked between Arne and me, then back to her husband. She yelled something in Icelandic, something I did not understand, and reached for the arrow in my hand.

Her magic armor flared. Its sigils and patterns rotated and folded, and it locked down around her body.

Arne raised his fist. "And you!" He pointed his finger at my face. "You didn't think to tell one of us that you'd checked out one of her books?"

The building shook again.

"Arne!" Dag yelled. "You need to—"

"I have cleansed this town of all rips!" Arne bellowed. "Not even ash remains."

His magic rippled and plumed very much as Dag's had at my house.

Out in the antechamber, the seasonal lines fell straight down into their places and nestled in as if they'd never lifted out in the first place.

"The Special Collection is vanquished," Arne yelled. "Every blossom has been pulled apart into its basic nitrogen and oxygen. Whatever is using that pathetic excuse of a fire spirit's equally pathetic spells to cross over into my town no longer has a gateway. It will not harm any more of my people."

"It is not that simple," Dag said. Her magic had collapsed around her into a shield I did not believe even Arne's anger could penetrate.

Arne slapped his hand over the wound in my arm. "I hereby seal all the dead with the blood of the dead."

My body stopped. Nothing flowed; nothing fired. All of time became my stoppage, and all of space became my lack of life.

I was no more than the desk, or the floor. I was uncaring in it all.

I'd sent a tracer through the portal in Rose's cottage. A marker that hit something on the other side. Something that mirrored me.

Now I mirrored it.

Dag fired a bolt of magic into my heart. "Damn it, Frank!"

And all that was me restarted. I gasped and backed into the desk.

"Have you learned nothing in your many centuries?" Dag spit at Arne. "You charged in and refused to allow our kind to return with our mundanes. How many elves died carrying your boats into the center of this continent?"

Arne's lips thinned.

"I may not have been here, but I know the tales, husband." Dag touched my forehead. "What happened when they found the tribes? You let loose your anger then, too." She took a step toward him. "I was here for that little display of bitterness."

Arne blinked rapidly. He inhaled sharply. "Remy leaves after the full moon. There will be no more magic from that island touching Alfheim." He slammed his fist down onto the counter. "Remy does not fear fire."

I stiffened.

Arne poked my chest. "My daughter and niece no longer live with you. They stay in The Great Hall."

He whipped his hand through the air before pointing at Dag. "If your father questions my decision, you tell him his concerns are not needed, nor will they be considered."

With that, the Elf King of Alfheim walked out of the Ramsey Mansion Library.

I wrapped my hand around my wound. It had already stopped bleeding, but it stung still. "There's more to this than closing portals," I called. There had to be.

Arne stopped in the antechamber, but he did not turn around, or answer.

"Leave Lizzy's cairn alone," I said. "Please." I didn't have the will to fight him anymore.

Arne walked away.

The Elf Queen watched him go. "Closing access is how you deal with a demon," she said. She sounded as stung and defeated as my arm felt. "It's the only way. My husband was correct in his actions."

"Maybe," I said. "You and I both know this isn't a simple vampiric demon we're dealing with."

She slapped the counter. "I shot at my husband."

So she'd felt the anger, too.

She pointed at the door. "This is not the first time his emotions have overflowed his vessel."

She blamed Arne. And here I'd thought it was the demon.

"Maura and Akeyla?" I asked.

"How is this better?" she asked more of the air than of me or Arne.

I backed against the counter. Had Arne actually destroyed all of Rose's artifacts? I should check for myself. Look. Touch. But in my heart I knew it would do no good.

Dag continued to stare at the open door. "They will never leave The Great Hall, Frank."

I hauled myself to my full height. "What?"

Dag nodded after Arne. "He hasn't lifted the banishment. He

cannot. It was declared by the other Kings." She tucked her bow into her quiver. "But he can sequester Maura and Akeyla here."

Arne could do the modern version of locking his daughter and granddaughter in a tower.

What could I say? How could I help? If I'd figured out what was going on sooner, would I have been able to save Maura and Akeyla from their fate?

Dag squared her shoulders. "It is done." She walked around the counter and hopped over the latched half-gate.

I stared at the door. Was there a way to fix this?

"Frank." Dag pointed at Tony's computer. "Help me with the security cameras. We can't have video of Arne tossing Tony around now, can we?"

No, we could not.

I nodded and did my best to help Dag clean up as much of this mess as she could.

CHAPTER 16

The workers across the lake started later than usual today, and the birds took advantage. A robin sang in the oak above my head. Somewhere along the shore, a crow called to his brethren. After a moment, another crow somewhere deep in the woods answered.

I sipped my oolong tea and stared out over the calm waters of my lake.

Two days and I hadn't heard one word from the elves. Two days since the Biterson brothers had vanished and the city had "temporarily" closed the Ramsey Mansion Branch Library. And three days since my dog had last come home.

Two God-forsaken days all alone in my house with only my thoughts and my noisy neighbors. At least the ghosts had also vanished.

No activity that looked suspiciously like a vampire attack. No sparks flying around Rose's Hill, either.

Arne, thankfully, left Lizzy's cairn alone, but I suspected that if he caught even a whiff of vampire, he would dismantle her marker with a bolt from the sky.

He wouldn't show his face here. He would simply destroy.

A saw started up across the lake. Banging followed. Above my head, the robin took wing. The sun warmed my deck, and I needed the heat before I left for this morning's trek through the trees in search of the emperor. I didn't want one of the construction guys stumbling across me, a walking corpse, out in the trees.

The sun, at least, was warm this morning, and my mat comfortable. A few more moments with my skin exposed to the sun's heat and I would return to something approaching human.

I sipped and swirled the last of my tea. *Stop feeling sorry for yourself,* the leaves said.

"Not helpful," I muttered, as if the leaves really had spoken to me. The only pattern in my cup looked more like my compost heap than any symbol.

I'd break Arne's neck if he touched the cairn. Rip his elf head off his elf body, magic be damned.

My mug shattered in my hand.

I blinked. What remained of my tea dripped onto my thigh. The mug's handle still curled around my fingers, but the rest landed as shards on my deck.

Arne, I thought, and threw the mug handle into the lake. I shook my hand. No cuts. No blood, just my body's disdain for an elf who thought he ruled everyone in Alfheim.

I stood. Droplets of tea clung to my knee and the shorts I'd thrown on this morning because of the workers.

Goddamned noise, I thought. Maybe they needed a lesson in manners, just like Arne.

Just like...

A ghost appeared at the edge of my deck, between me and the lake. A small ghost, a man, one I did not recognize yet who was eerily familiar.

He stood directly between me and the noisy neighbors.

He raised his hand and... the anger stopped. It did not recede, nor did it lessen, but it did cease churning.

As did the air around my head. The world became instantly stuffy. I tried to inhale.

What had been churning collapsed around my head into a suffocating mask. I pawed at the syrupy, thick magic. It clung to my fingers more like green slime than the normal light energy I usually saw. It dripped off my palm and smeared on my skin, but I got enough off to breathe again.

"Who are you?" I yelled. Why did he look familiar? "Why are you helping me?"

The ghost rubbed at his thick mop of curly brown hair, then at the tops of his ears. He waved his hand at me one more time, in short, staccato beats.

He vanished.

The magic slime shriveled. What still clung to my flesh fell off—as did my desire to snap Arne's neck and do harm to the workers across the lake.

A ghost of a familiar man had just cleaned the anger off my soul.

Normal anger remained—Arne's actions were infuriating—but the uncontrolled flailing, the chaotic fire from the start of my life, which for decades drove me to smash everything in my path, calmed. I knew how to control myself. I understood that my effects on the world were my own doing. I'd learned that lesson.

And suddenly, that control was no longer being overridden by *slime*.

We were not dealing with a simple demon, vampiric or not. This creature wielded spells.

Across the lake, someone yelled. Laughter followed. I rolled up my mat and walked back into my house.

Even if the elves did not want to talk to me, it was time for me to talk to them.

SUN WARMED the concrete under my feet. Cars drove by on the road. I raised my hand to part the glamour surrounding The Great Hall.

Nothing happened.

I walked forward, and again, the glamour did not part. I made it all the way to the hotel's dingy front entrance and tried the doors. They only rattled as if locked.

The elves—Arne in particular—had decided I was not to set foot in their realm. Nor were they answering their phones. Dag had not been in her office this morning, either.

I slapped the glass of the door. "Pettiness does not become you, Arne Odinsson!" I yelled. "Especially when I have information."

I resisted the urge to give the building the finger.

"Frank!"

I turned around. Gerard Geroux stood at the curb where I'd tried to part the glamour. He motioned for me to come back.

Gerard Geroux, like his brother, wasn't a large man in human form. He stood a couple inches shy of six feet, and though both he and Remy carried the broad shoulders and the square, chiseled features of their Norman ancestors, they watched the world from the dark eyes of a Celt. Both brothers' hair was as black as my own, but shimmered with copper highlights.

They'd given up their French Catholic heritage long ago, and now focused all their energy when dealing with other wolves toward containment and control, as opposed to shaming and maiming.

They were both scientists at heart, and from the stories they'd shared, it took them until the Scots showed up in the Red River Colony to fully comprehend what that meant. Taking a different path had given them as much peace as werewolves could have.

Without the Geroux brothers, many werewolves would have been put down. With them, the Alfheim Pack was a thriving, diverse community that had helped build the town toward the artistic mecca it was becoming.

Gerard nodded toward the glamour around The Great Hall. "He's not letting anyone in."

"Even you?" I asked.

Gerard's nose crinkled. He rubbed at its side, then shook his head. "It's full moon in three nights," he said.

I'd forgotten. Now was not the time for the elves to be pulling back their magic.

Gerard nodded toward The Great Hall. "It's okay. Arne and the other elves are still open to the pack. Nothing's going to go wrong."

Gerard did not seem to believe his own words. I clasped his arm. "How much did Ed explain?"

He hooked a thumb into a belt loop. "That something attacked you two on Rose's Hill." His frown deepened. "We're going out toward your place. Axlam will keep the pack closer together this time while Remy and I stay on the edges."

I nodded. "I was visited by another ghost."

Gerard stepped closer. "Who?"

"I did not recognize the man, though I felt I should have." I shook my head. I still could not place him. "He undid a spell."

"What?" Gerard looked up at The Hall as if he expected Arne to come striding out. "A ghost?"

"There's an anger," I said. "You saw it on me the last time I was here."

Gerard nodded.

"He broke it. Cleaned it. I'm not sure how to describe what happened other than to say he made it visible to me. It looked like slime. I was able to pull it off, and then it shriveled and died in the sun."

Gerard stared at the glamoured hotel for a long moment. "The moment Arne is willing to talk, I will tell him of this." He gripped my arm. "A magic the elves missed."

Gerard understood. This was not the first time he'd experienced the unexplainable. But he and Remy always figured out what was happening.

"I think so," I said.

Which was why he and the pack were still alive.

"Do you think the creature came through fully?" he asked. "Do you think it is still here?"

"Maybe," I said. "I don't know. If it did, it hasn't attacked anyone."

Gerard rubbed at his forehead. "It's only been two days."

"Yes." I pointed in the general direction of the library. "We haven't seen either Tony or Ivan, either." Vampires, when rudderless and afraid, attacked mundanes. It didn't matter how well-behaved they were overall; a frightened vampire responded to the world the same way as a cornered rat—it snarled and bit and frothed at the mouth.

"No, we have not," Gerard said. "They know we will hunt them if they run."

If anything scared a vampire, it was a hunting Alfheim Pack. "I think they're hiding."

Gerard sighed. "I suspect you are correct."

"The thing is, a vampiric demon would not hide," I said. "I'd think Arne closing its access points would terrify it."

"We have not sensed or scented any indication of a demon, Frank." He paused. "We've checked. Nothing."

So maybe Arne's closing of the portals did its job. "Be careful when the moon comes, anyway," I said.

Gerard pulled his sunglasses off the neck of his t-shirt and put them on his face. "We will keep an eye out for Marcus Aurelius, my friend. Axlam has tasked the pack with tracking your dog."

"Thank you." The wolves had a much better chance of finding my dog than I did. They all loved him, and would not harm him if they did find him.

I hoped. "Have any of the pack shown signs of excessive anger?"

Gerard shook his head. "No. It seems to be centered on you and the elves."

Me. Was being the epicenter good or bad? I did not know. "Just be careful."

"We will," Gerard said. "We will."

CHAPTER 17

Dag wasn't in her office at the Administrative Complex, but Ed was in his.

The Alfheim County Sheriff's Department, along with Alfheim's city police force, occupied the largest concrete slab at the end of the complex. Like the city offices, the building was well-manicured and framed by a wide assortment of industrial-looking shrubs and flowers. A huge, ironic, orange and black "No guns allowed on the premises" sign hung on the front entrance. The fact that the Sheriff's Department needed such an overt reminder to Alfheim's mundane citizens made me wonder about the wider world.

But I was not here to discuss the problems caused by random people. I was here to speak to Ed about magic slime, his family's safety, and the wolves.

Deep inside the building, past three separate defense check-points, I leaned against the frame of Ed's door. "I got another visit this morning," I said.

Ed waved me in. "Close the door," he said.

I twisted to cross his threshold—even normal three-foot door spans cause me some trouble—and closed the door behind me.

"A ghost?" he asked as he clicked closed a window on his computer screen.

I shook my head. "No one I recognized."

Ed leaned back in his chair. "A non-known visitation? Does that happen?"

I pulled out one of the chairs in front of his desk, but pushed it to the side when I realized it had arm rests. "It takes incredible magic to manifest a ghost for someone with whom the phantom has no geometry in common." I pulled forward one without rests. "I didn't see any magic around the ghost."

But me *not* seeing the magic was very much part of the bigger picture.

Ed nodded.

The chair groaned when I dropped my bulk onto it. "He did, though, show me the magic that has been clinging to me." I motioned with my hand to mimic pulling off of the anger. "It was like slime, Ed. Magical slime. The ghost did something to it. I couldn't see it before. I could after."

Ed leaned forward. "And you got it off?"

I rubbed the back of my neck. "I think so. I checked myself over before leaving the house."

Ed tapped a pen on his desk. "Like checking for magical ticks."

I would have chuckled if I'd felt up to it. "The elves won't talk to me."

Ed dropped the pen. "I know. Dagrun stopped by earlier. She's working on the inside." He rubbed his face. "Whatever that means."

I dared not ask, but I was beginning to wonder if we were about to have an elf coup on our hands. The last thing the town needed was a civil war between their King and their Queen, especially this close to Samhain.

"I swear whatever crossed over is trying to manipulate the elves." *Obviously*, I thought. Were Arne and Dag carrying the slime, too? But why? Because they were a threat? Because they held the power? Because they were elves?

All my questions seemed equally likely.

Ed pointed at me. "And you." He sat back again. "Pretty much you, brother."

I looked down at the floor. Yes, me. I was the epicenter. No getting around that. But why?

"Gerard says the pack has not sensed a demon," I said.

Ed picked up his pen again. "You had a ghost visitor this morning who revealed to you magic you could not see and that the elves did not sense." He pointed the pen at me. "The original access point got by both Maura and Mayor Tyrsdottir. The fire at the café looks like a gas leak only because the elves found no traces of non-Akeyla magic. You're seeing ghosts. And whatever attacked us at Rose's Hill hid itself from me."

Everything he said was true.

Ed tapped his pen on a report. "We've had an uptick in calls," he said. "Three dead or missing dogs last night."

Vampires feed on friendly beasts.

He held up his hand. "No sign of yours and no people missing, at least so far."

I nodded.

"Tony and Ivan may be feeding on people's pets. They're under control, but they're still vampires, and I bet they're as terrified as we are right now."

I nodded again.

"The wolves will be out with the moon." Ed looked up at the ceiling. "I asked the mayor to send a couple of trustworthy elves to the wolves' place. Enough to be on hand for when Gerard and Remy are out in the woods."

His family would be without guards once the wolves changed for the full moon. "I'll come over."

Ed frowned. He stared right at me for a long moment before speaking. "You are the epicenter of this, my friend. Forgive me if I don't want you near my kids right now."

His words stung worse than any of the dark magic we'd endured, but he did have a point.

A valid and legitimate point.

I didn't answer. I stood, instead. "Call if you get word on anything."

Ed moused open his tabs again. "Will do."

I walked toward the door.

"Frank," Ed said.

I turned around.

"Under any other circumstances I would have been honored to have you watch over my family."

I inhaled. "Thank you," I said, and walked out.

I DROVE out to Rose's Hill and parked my truck at the spot where Ed and I last saw Marcus Aurelius's tracks. The late afternoon sun threw warm shadows through the trees and stirred up the fresh, semi-sweet, semi-pulpy scent of living things. Leaves rustled. Birds called. The forest wasn't all that upset with Rose right now.

The hill wasn't visible from my spot in the ruts that made up the road. The forest floor rose on the other side of the trees, and an outcropping marked an area with elevations, but the hill itself was out of sight.

I had no desire to go up there, nor was I dumb enough to think visiting a dead witch's abode alone again was a good idea.

Better to wait until the elves decided they liked me again, and wanted to help, or for Gerard and Remy to serve as back-up.

Except I knew, deep down, that a part of Rose was still here, and that part wanted to help. Her remaining magic didn't feel malevolent. It didn't feel particularly benevolent, either, for that matter, but it did feel more alive than the flickering remains of a witch's magic should feel.

Perhaps I was reading into what had happened on the hill. Perhaps I wanted so badly to feel the good left of Rose's soul so much I made it up. Perhaps not. Either way, she did answer my questions as best as the dead could.

So many questions remained. So many clues that still seemed to serve no purpose. What did Ivan mean by borders and mixing? What purpose did he serve by giving me that book?

Why was I the epicenter?

I picked up a bag of Marcus Aurelius's favorite treats from the seat of my truck. "Here, boy!" I yelled, and walked into the trees.

A bird screeched. I looked up just as a bald eagle flew over. Her white head and tail gleamed in the sun, as did her huge yellow talons.

The elves considered birds of prey to be symbols of strength and luck, as did the Native Americans. I hoped they were both correct.

THREE HOURS of searching turned up zero signs of my dog. No signs of Tony or Ivan, either, or gnawed-on carcasses. No vampire marks. No demon signs. Just several pissed off raccoons, a fox, and a lot of leaf-strewn ground.

I drove my truck by the new construction just to get a better look at the progress. The sooner they got it done, the happier I'd be.

An empty, expensive sedan waited on the gravel next to the chrome and glass monstrosity, and a man I did not recognize talked to the foreman. The guy looked like any Cities tourist with his jeans and his craft brewery t-shirt, but had an air about him that said either owner or designer.

I waved as I drove by. The new man smiled and waved as if asking me to stop.

He jogged over. "Hello!" he said, and offered his hand through my open driver's side window. "I'm Aaron. Aaron Carlson."

He looked to be in his late forties, maybe early fifties, and had some gray peppered into his hair. A slight belly suggested he sat more for his work than the laborers building his new house. His face, though, looked younger.

"Frank Victorsson," I said.

We shook.

"You live across the lake, correct?" He pointed.

"Yep. That's me," I said.

"They're almost done with the exteriors," he said. "The noise will lessen soon."

I chuckled. "Good."

He chuckled, too. "Our youngest just started college." He grinned. "And I'm semi-retiring. We thought a lake house would be nice."

"It's lovely here," I said.

"God, isn't it?" He stared out at the trees. "Here," he said, and pulled a card from his pocket. "My cell's on the back, in case you know anyone who might want to take care of the place when we're not here."

He smiled.

I took the card. "Aaron Carlson, attorney at law. Specializing in immigration, defense, and personal injury law," it said.

"You're a lawyer?"

"Yeah," he said. "My wife does intellectual property."

"Ah," I said.

"Well," Mr. Carlson, attorney at law, said, "We're hoping the place will be ready by Christmas." He looked almost forlorn. Almost.

I extended my hand again. "Nice to meet you, Mr. Carlson."

"Call me Aaron. Please."

"Will do, Aaron," I said.

"Interesting tattoos you have," he said, and pointed at my head. "Is that Yggdrasil?"

One of my protection tattoos had a real-world base that was, in fact, the world tree. "It is," I said.

"You *have* to come by once we're in. Our middle daughter is working toward an art degree and she will grill you about the design."

I wasn't sure being "grilled" by a lawyer's artist offspring sounded like a good time, but being neighborly often meant putting up with annoying children.

"Will do," I said one more time.

He patted the door of my truck. "Good to meet you, Mr. Victorsson."

"Good to meet you too, Mr. Carlson," and waved one last time as I made my way around the lake and to my home.

CHAPTER 18

Another day of searching for Marcus Aurelius led to nothing but more dashed hopes. Three days he'd been gone now, with no signs. The wolves would look for him tomorrow night, but my worry had blossomed into something cold and shaky in my gut.

I'd lost animals before. Horses, an endless number of dogs, a few cats, goats, and a parrot. But losing the emperor felt different.

Ed had called mid-afternoon to tell me he had three more calls the night before, including a ripped-apart cow.

My loyal, faithful hound might be out there, somewhere, hiding in a hollow from vampires and a demon.

I put bowls of clean water and food out on the deck just in case. The raccoons would eat the food by morning, but if Marcus Aurelius did come back, he'd at least have something.

The sunset spread reds and oranges over the lake. Most of the work on the Carlsons' house had been interior today, with thankfully less noise. Workers still toiled inside, and must have either gotten the house connected to the grid or the solar panels and batteries set up, because the entire house was lit up like a Christmas tree.

I unrolled my mat and took up my usual morning place on my

deck. A little evening meditation might help calm my faithful companion, fear.

The moon peeked out over the tops of the trees. One more night and she'd be full—and the wolves would run the woods. And likely one more night without my dog.

I closed my eyes and counted my breath in, then counted as I slowly exhaled out. I would not mourn. He might yet make his way home, and I would continue my search. The wolves might find him tomorrow.

But it was hard.

I looked over my shoulder at the wide French doors and the silent kitchen beyond. Akeyla should be helping with dinner and chatting about her day.

My house, once again, was more silent than my poor soul could tolerate.

The moon stood out as a massive orb opposite the final deep reds and purples of the setting sun. Across the way, behind the glass, someone walked back and forth in front of Carlson's view of the lake. Several of the lights switched off.

Two of the workers walked out of the building and to their trucks. Another light switched off until only the room behind the big window remained on.

The ghost appeared again—the unrecognized man from a few days ago.

He manifested directly between me and my neighbors as a small, round man with curly hair and a hawkish nose.

He tilted his head and blinked his eyes just as the moon threw a glowing path from his back to the Carlson house.

I dared not move. Dared not to upset the geometry of his placement in the world, and mine, and the shining, bright line connecting us to neighbors I wasn't sure I liked.

"Who are you?" I asked. Ed was correct; he had to be someone I knew.

The ghost stuck out his tongue and silently hissed.

"Ivan?" Was I looking at the man Ivan was before he turned? Small, troll-like but not mean. Bookish, and perhaps slightly magical?

But Ivan was a vampire. Was I looking at the ghost driven from his form by the possessing demon-spirit?

"I don't understand, Ivan." Why would the ghost of a vampire offer information?

Why did any ghost offer information? Why did they manifest at all? I glanced around Ivan's human ghost at the path of moonglow.

A black shadow moved across the Carlson's lakeshore.

I stood up. Ivan vanished. Across the lake, the shadow slowed, turned, and pointed at me.

I grabbed my cell phone off the deck rail and ran for the shore. It'd take me seven minutes if I took my truck. Running the eastern shoreline, I could do it in five, as long as I didn't twist my ankle. Swimming, I could probably do three or four, but I'd be fighting wet on the other side.

I ran the shore.

The shadow extended upward from below the window as if it had tentacles, then pulled back to its blob of a body. In the house, the last workers stopped as if listening.

They didn't appear nearly as alarmed as they should have been.

I dialed Arne. His voice mail answered. "It's at the house across the lake."

I hung up, dialed Dag, and left the same message.

Ed answered just as I dodged into the first reed patch. "It's here," I said.

"What? At your place?" He yelled at his wife over his shoulder.

Mud squished into my boots as I picked my way closer to dry ground. "At the new house across the lake. There are workers still in the building. I'm halfway around the shore."

"Jesus, Frank—"

I tripped on a log and dropped my phone into the water. It glowed long enough for me to scoop it out before it sank too deep, but it sputtered and died in my hand.

I swore under my breath and did my best to stay silent. The creature might have better hearing than most, or it might sense my anger. I did my best to center and stay as calm as possible, and to continue moving.

I tucked the phone into my pocket. Nothing I could do about it now.

The shadow inched up the side of the house toward the grand window as if scaling the siding. It moved more like an insect than anything remotely human. "What the hell are you?" I whispered.

I couldn't be sure it was the same creature that had attacked Ed and me at Rose's Hill. Not until I got close. But my gut said yes.

My gut also said I needed to run in the opposite direction.

I snuck out of a second set of reeds as best I could and then around one of the worker's trucks. I couldn't see the shadow well, nor could I see magic around it. But I smelled ash.

Rose's ash, from her hill. From her home. This was the creature that had attacked Ed and me.

Arne's attempts to keep it at bay had failed.

It stood at the house's foundations with its hands on its hips, watching the people up above. A woman walked over to the window and looked out, stepped into the room again, then stepped back to the window.

She must have sensed something, probably in the same way that Ed had sensed it before. The two workers with her didn't seem to care.

The shadow creature pointed up at the woman. "She looks tasty," he said.

I froze. So much for stealth.

The creature laughed. "You are not a man capable of sneaking in any sense of the word, dear son of Victor."

A large, black bird landed on the house's roof. The animal cocked its head and spread its crow-like wings, but stayed silent.

The shadow pointed at the bird, then touched his ash-swirling finger to his face. "Quiet," he said.

I looked up at the crow, then at the creature. "What are you?" I asked again.

"You dropped your phone," he said. "Did you think to bring a flashlight?" He pointed at the woman. "They'll turn off the lights when they leave."

How could I be so dense? I had no way of holding off the creature. None. But at least for the moment the people in the house were safe.

"You anchored yourself here before Arne closed the portals," I said.

The creature laughed. "I love how elves think they know everything about magic."

"You are not a simple demon," I said. He was too articulate to be an unthinking creature. He'd traveled through The Land of the Dead an already fully-formed vampire.

Was Dag correct? Was he an assassin? "Which clan sent you?" I asked.

He continued to stare up at the window. "Clans?" He sighed. "Please."

He'd done what we'd suspected Maura's ex was trying to do—walked through The Land of the Dead. "You already have a body. That's how you anchored yourself here." No other explanation fit the shadow creature in front of me.

He laughed. "And you? Aren't you simply possessing a body built by science instead of offered up by magic?"

I stepped out from behind the truck. "I am not a demon." My father's words held no truth. "I am, like all non-magicals, the product of the life fueling my form."

The creature laughed. "Aren't we all?"

He appeared directly in front of me. Up in the house, someone laughed. A light moved, and the creature, who had been backlit, now had a beam of light filtering around his side and through the ash.

He looked down at my face. This thing, this creature, stood a good five inches taller than me, an already monstrous giant. But unlike me, he watched the world from icy, honey-colored eyes set in an unscarred, strong-jawed face.

An unnaturally handsome face framed by wide, lovely brown curls. His teeth glowed in the slight light, too alabaster and too predatory. I was most definitely face-to-face with a vampire—a vampire unlike any other I had met or knew of.

He winked and stepped back. Like me, his wide shoulders fit proportionally with his huge frame. Also like me, he would have a difficult time with the mundane architecture of the world—doors, vehicles, clothing. But this creature had no connection to the mundanes other than to feed on them.

"I will tell you the truth, son of Victor. I feel I owe you that much," he said.

"Why?" I should stay silent, but the more he spoke, the more information I gained. And if he was like all people coming out of isolation —magical or otherwise—he would be particularly talkative. Best to use what advantage I had.

His ash cloak pulled inward. It tightened and settled, and folded down onto his frame like a well-cut, well-made suit. This demonic vampire stood at the base of a new house dressed in dapper death.

I had been correct, he was traditionally handsome, but I was incorrect about the scarring. Along his neck and up toward his ear, a fine tree-like—or perhaps bolt-like—scar fanned out over his skin. Unlike my old and puckered scars before they'd healed and lessened, his looked smooth—more a discoloration than anything else. His scars would not disgust a woman.

They could be a tattoo. I had a tree on my scalp. He might as well. But if his was Yggdrasil, it was a dark and twisted, deathly version of what a world tree should be.

His eyes narrowed. "I will tell you the truth, son of Victor, because I wish to."

"Then speak," I said.

He clasped his hands behind his back and returned to watching the woman and the workers. "I had been watching for an opening into this place," he said. "Waiting. The elven protections here are strong." He sniffed. "I even tried via that dead witch's books. I figured the two vampires here would help."

He tugged at his black ash cuffs. "They did not." He shook his head.

"Not their fault. That witch left as many protections as the elves have laid."

The woman stepped away from the window. The creature walked backward, to keep a sightline on her. "But there is a geometry to the universe, don't you agree? A particular set of lines and angles that one must respect." He waved his hand. "They can be obtuse at times, the angles. They can make passage painful unless you have a light to guide you."

I did not answer.

"It's scientific, really." He chuckled. "Navigation. That fire spirit added just enough spark to allow me to see the slicing of the shifting planes and points. But, son of Victor, can you guess what gave me the beacon I needed? The glaringly bright light that illuminated my course?"

The notebook. "Rose's book was—"

He chortled and pointed his finger at my nose. "That book? Oh, no, my dear brother. That notebook *was* blank. It still is. The only thing it does is reflect into the real world any light in The Land of the Dead."

The flower... "So that flower was a manifestation of the firelight caused by Maura's ex?"

He touched the side of his nose and winked.

"But..." But Maura's ex wasn't nearly good enough to light a path into Alfheim for this creature.

"But what?" he asked.

"But a tracer is bright enough." A tracer allows magic to home in on a location.

I never thought it might work both ways.

He clapped his hands. "Yes!" Then spread his arms wide. "I *called* to you! We are connected, you and I. And you answered."

I let him in?

"And once here, I turned that witch's spells to my advantage." The ash around him lifted up and wiggled, then dropped back toward his body. "The soot of the dead will cloak its wearer from most magic of the living." He grinned. "But only if you are dead."

No, he was not a simple vampiric demon, or even one complex. He was something with an understanding of dark magic beyond that of the elves.

"I called to you with the voice we both know so well." He pointed at the crow. "The rage. The anger. I sent my friends and I had them glue it to you, to amplify the signal."

The crows. The ravens. The *slime*.

He pointed a well-manicured finger toward my chest. "I needed the beacon of your pain. I needed to feel your anger at being forced to awaken inside a body polluted by death."

No, I thought. *No*. My father died shortly after he built me.

"I've been looking for you, *brother*," he said.

What did my father do?

My brother sneered.

And my brother punched me in the face.

CHAPTER 19

I blacked out.

Or I blacked *in*. I entered something—somewhere—that was not my neighbor's property. Somewhere utterly human.

Two hundred years is beyond a mundane's perspective. What happened a decade ago is ancient history; what happened two centuries before was to be romanticized. So my pre-Victorian origins were, to most living humans, a flurry of uptight clothes, clockwork industry, well-mannered aristocrats, and imperialism.

My father had been a man of means. He had the fortune to build himself a well-stocked laboratory. He understood his letters well enough to collect and consume other great men's opinions about science. But like so many of the well-mannered imperialists of the time, he believed himself to be more important to the natural order of the world than he truly was.

I remembered waking into a thick world, one soot-covered and coal-infused. The sour smell of unfresh humans and their wastes caught by the Alpine winds and carried away to other, uncared-about places. The noise of carriages and the clomp of horse hooves on paving stones in the village below his manor home.

This memory-place into which my "brother" knocked me was the world of my wakening—yet it was not. Soot, coal, stink—they were all here. Steel and ice, as well.

I'd never tried to explain to the elves what had happened to me, or how it was that I came to be. Two hundred years and the memories have faded to the point that I now carry more memories of remembering my pain than I do of the pain itself.

The distance was what allowed me to heal the anger. When I began to remember the remembering more than the moments of agony and the madness themselves, it gave me a flowing river between the present and the past. A distraction of gurgling, cleansing water which, when I allowed it to, separated me from the worst of the pain.

My "brother" had been bridging that river for the last few days with his magical slime, and when he punched me in the face, he lifted me up and dropped me on the opposite shore.

I landed face-down in horse dung and mud. A nearby woman laughed. A man spoke unintelligible snark. Heels clicked cobblestones. Gaslights hissed and flickered.

A fog rolled into an Edinburgh night.

Scotland, not Germany, yet cold, crisp air, filled with the same soot and fumes. Same cruel human condition. Same uncaring within which I'd gasped to life.

To the side, in both directions, a cobblestone street stretched between brick and wood buildings. I was on a hill, or the world tilted. I did not know which. But the building in front of me, a rickety and ugly tenement with more broken windows than not, rose into the night's blackness. And at the very top, in one single, small window, a blazing flare of artificial light.

No lightning. No storm, this time.

How far up were they? Five stories? To my mind, it seemed to be two hundred, one for each of my years. Yet I knew what my father did. I smelled the acerbic bath and the bitter fumes.

He stitched together bits.

I started as bits—cut up, sliced apart, and set too distant from joint to joint for my body to talk to itself and to function correctly.

This was what I never spoke of with the elves. I never thought they would understand. My body had once been bits. I never formed as a whole. I never built my own entirety. I started as a jumble with fingers disconnected from my hands. With guts unwound. I started unmade, only to be remade.

And though over my years I have come to integrate what was never meant to be integrated, my size is not correct and some parts of my brain still believe myself to be those original bits.

Mostly in dreams. Mostly combined with uncontrolled falling, or chaos, or drowning. But *not* being right has always been part of me, or more precisely an un-part bit of me.

I was stretched. I was just a little too far apart to be steady. I was unsettled.

And there was nothing at all I could say or describe to give another person a sense of what it meant to be made of the parts of others. Nothing I could do beyond causing an equal amount of fear.

And fear becomes terror. And terror becomes anger.

But I was no longer that patchwork thing. I could not be that monster. I was Frank Victorsson, a man with friends. A man with a community. I had no reason to fear or to rage. I was no longer bits.

My father never understood. My father screamed and cursed me and called me demon. I was not the child he wanted and his focus had been on his disdain for that which did not meet his expectations. He could have helped me find what life I could inside my lack of perfection. He did not.

Because my father had been blinded by his own self-absorption.

So blind that he found his way to Edinburgh where he set up another lab. A better one based in one of Europe's centers of innovation. And one in the heart of a land that did not lack magic.

Up there, in that lab, the light switched from artificial to magical. Down in the gutter where I lay, the mud turned prophetic. The horseshit, the end product of nature's anger.

My father had added something to his formula for binding bits together—but he'd also started with stronger bits. With pieces used to being chopped apart and thrown to the four corners of the world.

For his second attempt, in his immeasurable hubris, my father's patchwork had been a quilt of vampire corpses.

A bolt hit a rod above the tenement, but not a natural bolt. This one came from The Land of the Dead.

I gagged and vomited onto the remembered cobblestones, and my mind asked the one horrible question, the one that chilled my gut and swelled my self-hatred: "Did you at least kill him?"

My brother, this monster born of science and magic and evil, squatted in front of my place in the dirt. And my brother grinned with his razor fangs. "Of course I killed him. Someone had to," he said. "If I hadn't killed him, how could he haunt you now?"

How could any of my ghosts haunt me? Lizzy. My father. Ivan. They all came with their warnings, but my geometry was wrong. I was pulled and snapped and stretched too far.

"Thank you," I said.

My brother touched the tattoo of Yggdrasil on the side of my scalp. "You wear the world tree, brother called Frank. You wear the balance of life and death, of knowledge and magic. You have been blessed by elves and gods alike."

He stood. "I know you feel that you cannot describe our unsettled-ness." He looked up at the now-dark window. "I will, then."

Once again, he straightened his ash-made cuffs. "Death is a process, brother. Dissolution takes time. For most, it is what it is—a state change. But for others, for the tortured and the murdered, there is no beginning of the process. They come into their story in the middle." He watched a couple walk by. "More dramatic that way."

He kicked a pebble and it bounced off my arm. "Do you understand the physiology of surprise? Of the sudden shift of attention and the spike in adrenaline? The firing of nerves?"

I shook my head.

He shrugged. "It makes prey tastier." He pointed at me. "It also makes a consciousness all that more aware of dying. All that more aware of its own terror and the pain of the end."

The pain and the terror were the same thing. The need to run and vomit and scream at the same time a body was only capable of freezing in place. Nothing hurt more. Not a knife wound. Not being hit by a hammer, or breaking a bone. Being torn to bits, dissolving, was the ultimate, overriding agony.

No wonder so much witch magic was based on death. No wonder my brother used The Land of the Dead as his conduit—besides its ease of access, it gave him both energy to manipulate and a freedom from caring about its costs.

Not that a vampire would care anyway. "Are you one vampiric demon, or the stitched together bits of many?"

He blinked as if I'd handed him the most novel of puzzles. "Does it matter?" he asked.

Probably not to him, but it did to me. "You are only my brother if you understand the question."

Magic flared through his ash cloak. Red, raging magic. Magic pulled from this somewhere-realm dream—from him, I suspected.

Behind him, the strolling woman screamed.

My brother kicked me in the head.

CHAPTER 20

T he woman screamed and screamed and screamed.
My back and neck arched. My jaw opened and my shoulders dropped back. The top of my head hit the real ground and the real moon trail across the lake spread toward my home as an upside down, painted-on glow.

I was on the ground, on my back, with a hump or a log or something else pressing up into my mid-back.

Except the log was soft. And a woman screamed.

I gasped and rolled to the side—and directly over a face. A dead face. A still-warm man whose arms had not yet stiffened. A familiar face that I could not quite place.

I checked his pulse just in case. Nothing.

The woman screamed again.

I looked up. The woman who had been inside the house stood on the pebbles up the shore, toward the house. Two workers flanked her protectively, as if I was about to charge. She flicked up her cell phone and took a picture.

My brother did this. I looked down at the dead man again. "Do any of you know who this is—" It dawned on me where I'd seen the corpse's features. He was one of the two idiots who had recorded Maura and Akeyla at the café.

"Call 911!" I said. "Go back inside! The man who did this is… subtle." I couldn't tell them the truth. "He's fast. You are all in danger." I looked around, but all evidence of my brother had vanished.

"You did this, dude," one of the workers said. "You snapped that guy's neck."

"What?" I poked at the body's shoulder. His neck had most definitely been snapped. "I did not." I'd been in an alternate state. A magical viewing. Not *here*.

"You're the neighbor," the woman said. "Aaron told me about you."

I didn't know her name. I hadn't asked when I talked to her husband. "I didn't do this," I said.

Sirens wailed not too far away, and blue and red flashing lights popped through the trees.

Ed was on his way.

Ms. Carlson turned her phone's light onto my chest. The angle and backscatter gave me a better view of her face and the faces of the workers than I suspect she intended.

Every part of her face had rounded in surprise. "I witnessed—" She stopped cold as if someone had ahold of her throat.

"Mrs—" said one of the men, then he, too, stopped talking.

My body wanted to jump up. I wanted to move, to meet Ed, but like Ms. Carlson and the workers, an unseen magic held me fast.

A shadow swirled, and my brother appeared between Ms. Carlson and the worker on her left. He sniffed at her neck as if inhaling the perfect aroma of a brilliantly-prepared meal. "Mundanes," he said, then vanished again.

I gasped as his magic released my body. Ms. Carlson dropped her hand to her side and took the beam of her phone's light with it. Neither she nor the men made any attempt to run away, or to talk, or to do anything. All three stood like mannequins.

Ed cut the siren as he pulled his cruiser between the worker's two trucks and onto the properties beachfront. The cruiser's lights continued to pulse out headache-inducing red and blue flashes as Ed exited his vehicle.

He held his service weapon pointed down, but still in hand and ready. "Frank!" he yelled. "Explain!"

Ms. Carlson pointed at me. "He killed that man!" she screamed. "We saw it! He killed him right there on my beach!"

"Ed! Get back in your car! He's here." My brother might take control of Ed, too.

"Frank..." he said, as he raised his weapon.

"I think they're thralled," I said.

Ed yelled a rapid stream of Latin. Church words hadn't worked last time, though these seemed different in cadence and structure.

"Oh... your friend found some new passages," my invisible brother whispered into my ear. "How modern of him."

He vanished. The feel of his presence vanished. Shadows brightened. The squinting induced by the pulsing of Ed's cruiser lights lessened. But Ms. Carlson continued to yell and point.

"I'm a lawyer!" she shouted. "Detain him!"

Ed lowered his weapon. He looked from the frantic mundanes to me, then back at the mundanes. "Do you have video on that phone of yours?" He held out his hand.

She tucked her phone into her pocket. "We do this correctly and according to the law."

Ed holstered his gun. "Cooperate or I'll charge *you* with obstruction."

"He's a murderer!" Ms. Carlson screeched.

Ed raised his hands. "Calm down." He walked toward me. "Frank, I may need to put you in the cruiser."

I looked back at Ms. Carlson. She gyrated around like a puppet on strings. The worker next to her stood completely still. "Where's the other guy?" There had been two.

A pop, and a bullet whizzed by my cheek.

I dropped low just as the man stepped out from behind his truck, hands and large handgun raised.

"Lower that weapon now!" Ed shouted. "*Now!*"

The man's face looked as lifeless as the corpse's. "He's thralled, Ed."

Ed swore. "Can you make it to the pallet over there?"

A stack of roofing material stood about halfway between me and the house. "Probably." I was fast, but I was also a large target. A bullet was unlikely to kill me, but it would hurt, and might incapacitate me for an hour or so if he hit an organ.

The man continued to lurch toward me.

"I don't want to shoot him," Ed said.

I ran for the pallet. Another bullet screamed by my arm, and another by my back, but I made cover without a physical wound.

But I was in the shadows, and the shadows held my family. The ghost of my father stood inches from my side. Even dead, Victor Frankenstein walked the world better integrated than his son.

"What did you do?" I asked.

He allowed his hubris to be all that he was. He was an empty vessel, my father. He had always been nothing more than a shell in need of validation. Was he man enough to justify his fortune? Was he intelligent enough to never be forgotten?

Was he god enough to cheat life itself and make a creature utterly, mercilessly his?

I failed. I lumbered. I terrified. I was too ugly to be a beautiful child. So my father, unable and unwilling to find a more sating and nutritious filling for his vessel, went back to his addiction: his self-absorption and pride. And my father built a new me—a better me—from the parts of creatures who had died and refused to stay dead.

My father looked up at the almost-full moon, inhaled deeply without inhaling at all, and leaned toward me. *Run*, he mouthed, and slid away along the lines and curved paths into The Land of the Dead.

Ed shouted at the thralled man. Ms. Carlson screeched. And in front of me, in the blackness between the trees, Lizzy's silver and gray muzzle beckoned.

I ran for the dark forest in front of me.

CHAPTER 21

Sheets of magic lifted from Lizzy's ghost fur and danced in the night air between the trees. The woods cooled, and the branches crackled. The scent of sun shifted toward the thicker, foggier silver of deep night. Humidity touched my nose and throat, and damp moss the soles of my boots.

I followed a phantom of moon magic deep into the primordial forests at the heart of a continent. Squirrels watched me from their hollows. An owl hooted from the treetops. Birds were here, somewhere, hiding in their nests and awaiting the return of sun and warmth. Some plants opened their blossoms to the moon, others, like the birds, hid away instead.

Most creatures in the woods understood the night. They knew if they were equipped for the dark, or if they should huddle and wait it out.

Night, day, it did not matter. I was now, and had always been, out of my element. This world was for the living. I was a man made of dead puzzle pieces.

Was my brother as disjointed as I? Each step, for me, was the coordinated effort of legs and blood vessels that only knew each other because they'd been locked in the same room for two hundred years.

They fought at times; they laughed and danced at others. But they were not singular.

My meditations helped. I learned the basics of psychology and biology when I went to college. My education somehow allowed me to follow the trails into a spotty understanding of what my father had done. But my joints still crackled. My back did not always align. My breathing did not always do what it was supposed to do, and I met each morning with more death on my skin than warmth.

I was alone, yet I was never alone with myself.

My brother killed one of his minions and thralled others to frame me for the murder. Not as a way to remove me from the picture—no, Ed would deal with this issue. My brother murdered to feed his vampiric need for mayhem and chaos that was as strong as his need for blood.

Lizzy's ghost stayed just out of reach as she led me through the brambles.

"Where are you leading me?" I asked.

She looked over her shoulder and noiselessly barked. Then my long-dead hound, the beautiful beast who once walked at my side, who pulled my sled and led the way because there always had to be forward movement—*always*—leaped a log into a clearing and vanished into a spray of magic sparks and ribbons.

A column of glow dropped through the air to a patch of wild-flowers at the center of the clearing. Fireflies rose from the flowers like tiny sparks of magic—green and lovely and more alive than a flame could possibly be.

The clearing itself wasn't much more than twenty feet across, and the flower patch no more than seven. A sweet, honeydew-like scent increased and decreased with the breeze, as did the fluttering of the fireflies.

I looked up. The moon hung directly overhead. A perfectly perpendicular shaft of light dropped directly into the flowers.

I looked down at the ground.

Rose stood in the flowers. Rose, with her tight black curls and her large, bear-brown eyes. My lovely, good Rose.

She wore a fluttering white gown of translucent fabric, one that bared her arms but covered her breasts, torso, and legs with tucks and gathers. Her hair had been pulled back from her face and tied into a knot at her crown.

My Rose looked more goddess than ghost.

"Are you real?" I asked.

Slowly, she blinked. And just as slowly, she smiled.

"I'm so sorry, Rose," I said. "I'm sorry I brought you here. I'm sorry I allowed you so much agony. No one deserves to die writhing in insanity."

Rose looked up at the moon. "I do not have much time, Father," she said.

She spoke? Ghosts did not speak.

"I'm not a ghost. Not like Lizzy or your father." She twirled around. "I cleansed myself of the pain and that cleansing brought me one last time to you."

She extended her hand.

I took a step into the clearing.

"I wish I had time to explain," she said. "To give you a sense of this magic."

I reached out for her hand.

Rose slapped her hands over my ears and dug in her fingers. She floated up like a movie phantom, her dress billowing off bits of white, gauzy smoke as if a strong wind blew through the clearing. But we were alone with only the breeze and the moonlight.

She hung there, in the magic of the universe, at eye level with me. No real hands gripped the sides of my head. No warmth, no skin, no sweat or dirt or the joy of living. Just a tiny portion of what once was my dear Rose.

I sensed the lack of depth to the magic around me. This Rose was all that shimmered, and nothing that toiled. This was a reflection that had been put through filters to remove the grease, and the filth, and the pain. Like Ivan's ghost had done for me, she had been cleansed of the slime.

This Rose was more for me than for her.

137

She smiled again. "Maybe," she said. "Maybe not." She floated closer. "Since when has the world been that simple?"

Nothing was simple when magic was involved.

"I left you everything you need." She pointed over my shoulder in the direction of her hill. "You need to clean off the ash, too, Father."

The moon's beam moved, or the world moved under the beam, and Rose disappeared.

"Rose?" I swiped at the air. "Damn it! Why are spirits so vague?"

I wanted to rip up all the flowers, but wanton destruction would help no one, and I knew deep in my heart that killing things—even blossoms—was the last thing Rose would want me to do. She'd spent her life fighting the black urges. I had spent *my* life fighting those same urges. They pulled from different wells, her urges and mine, but their effect was the same.

Different engines, same outcome. Agony had a way of destroying no matter its cause.

"*What* did you leave, Rose?" I yelled. "Size, shape, and color?" *Animal, mineral, or vegetable?* I thought.

No answer from the night or the spirit world. No call from The Land of the Dead. Only my own breathing and the chirps of well-hidden frogs.

But I knew: She wanted me to trek to her hill in the dark, without my phone, or a weapon, or a flashlight. Or my dog.

I rubbed my forehead. I knew which way to go in a general sense. But this clearing was new to me, and I didn't quite have my bearings. "Should I trust my instincts?" I asked the breeze.

Which set of instincts? The ones from the brain in my head, or the ones from the piecemeal body it inhabited? Or perhaps from the piecemeal, gifted magic tattooed onto my body.

I rolled over my arm and stared at the tracer tattoos marked from my wrist to my elbow. They also shimmered with moonglow. And Earth magic. And family. "Lot of good you've done," I mumbled.

What good are protection enchantments if they don't protect? But the ones I carried did protect me—they just protected me from *living* magic.

I touched the tattoo of Yggdrasil on the side of my head. Arne had made no secret that he considered me of many realms, and that he believed the tree fit my soul.

But the tree was life. I rubbed at my hair. Perhaps someday I would understand.

I never realized how little of vampire magic I saw. Tony and Ivan—as well as every other vampire I have had the displeasure of meeting—did not exude any sense of the magical. They oozed metastasized addiction. Nothing a vampire did was of its own free will. A vampire served its bloodlust, and thus its demon.

Yet that bloodlust gave its demon its own special, dark anti-magic. And my brother had found a way to control it.

My father had tried to build a better mundane with me. Larger, faster, quicker at learning book knowledge—that was me. But the perfection that was supposed to be me had been decanted into a faulty vessel.

So he had made a new larger-faster-quicker vessel from parts with a wholly different imperative. Because of hubris.

"I should have chased you, Father," I said. "I should have carried you with me into this new land." If I had strapped him to my sled, the elves would have put a fear of all the gods and of magic itself into him. And perhaps he would have found some humility.

Fireflies danced over the meadow's white blossoms. I looked up at the moon, then out at the small pops of green flitting through the air. Time to make my way to Rose's Hill.

CHAPTER 22

Every breath was a boundary crossed. Every moment one staved off death was a step into another realm. The big difference between living and a state of death was caring about the transition.

Rose's Hill breathed, but it did not live. The ash reflected, but the ash did not care. And somewhere in it Rose had left me "all I needed."

On top of the hill, the sense of peaks and valleys remained, as did the otherworldly calm. The realm into which she'd shunted her cottage was a moment without a boundary, a place one could not cross out of with ease.

It was a borderland on the edges of death, a slow place where the labor of living began to give way to the endless uncaring. A shadowed place of ashes and vampires.

The cottage had manifested once again as a solid phantom. The door opened like a real door, and the little house smelled of Rose's herbs and minerals—thyme, sage, salt, sulfur. No heat rose from the hearth's stones, and no sighs from the sleeping loft. The stepping stone papers that had ignited a path to the portal were back to their original form. No portal shimmered.

I was utterly alone.

And there, on the floor in the center of the cottage, sat the only thing not made of its own remains: The blank notebook.

I walked directly to it, picked it up, and walked out of the cottage in one swift movement.

The door slammed behind me and the entire structure—the entire frozen moment Rose's cottage occupied—vibrated.

For a second, I considered trying the door. What if it was locked? What if I'd taken the wrong artifact? Would I be able to get back inside if I needed to?

But these were all the questions a trap used to spring its jaws, so I did not. I flipped through the notebook's pages instead.

Nothing. No writing. No notes or drawings, not even a smudge, just like before.

I slammed it shut and flipped it over to look at the spine.

A dagger fell out.

I flipped it over and opened it again. Still blank. I rotated it and shook.

Nothing.

The notebook obviously had a mind of its own. I tucked it under my arm and picked up the dagger—if it could be called a dagger.

A bolt of energy ran up my arm, but the dagger did not force me to drop it. Whatever magic it possessed, it seemed okay with me touching it.

The object was more a stake than anything else, and one forearm-length carved piece of hardwood. The hilt and guards had been stained a deep red, and the grip wrapped in leather.

A shallow channel ran down the center of the blade and had been domed over by what appeared to be thin and fragile glass. The liquid inside glimmered with magic.

Someone had added a break-on-impact vessel full of a potion—holy, perhaps—to what appeared to be a vampire-killing weapon.

I tested the edge.

It cut into my finger. For wood, it was exceptionally sharp. Yes, this wooden knife was meant to stop the heart of a fiend.

"Thank you, Rose," I said. "Thank you from the bottom of the bits that make up my heart." Though retrieving this artifact had been much too easy. I understood how magic worked. Balance must be retained. The elves and their brethren had a connection to all things earth, air, water, and fire, and could shift elements to achieve that balance. A witch's faulty connection caused breakdowns.

And then there was me, a man who carried the enchantments of others. I had no intrinsic way to achieve a balance.

Which meant this dagger came with a price. "So be it," I muttered. I'd pay whatever price magic demanded to remove my murderous brother from Alfheim. This time, I'd do what was necessary.

The sunrise peeked over the trees as I climbed back down the hill with dagger and book in hand.

I wasn't surprised when I heard a large vehicle picking its way along the tracks that led to Rose's Hill.

Hiding seemed the best option, but hiding would do no good against the elf whose magic flared out in front of the vehicle like the sun itself.

Dagrun had borrowed someone's SUV and had come looking for me.

She pulled up and cut the engine. "Get in," she said, and slapped the doorframe.

Who was I to argue with the Queen of Alfheim? I opened the passenger door and hopped into the SUV.

Dag glanced at the notebook and the dagger. "Where did *that* come from?" She eyed the dagger suspiciously when I held it up.

"It fell out of the book." No reason to hide the truth from her.

She took her hand off the ignition. "Leave it here."

I set it down on top of Rose's notebook once again. "I think Rose sent it to me. I think I'm supposed to use it against the creature."

Dag crinkled her nose as she inhaled. "I have never, in all my centuries, seen anything like that knife, but I have smelled such weapons." She started up the SUV. "It doesn't smell right, Frank."

"Not right as in *evil*, or not right as in *not elf magic*?" Because both options presented their own set of problems. "The only magic I see is in the potion sloshing in the vessel here." I held up the dagger again.

The Elf Queen of Alfheim dropped all shreds of glamour she carried. All of it, and not just the mundane disguise she wore on a daily basis. In the blink of an eye, Dagrun Tyrsdottir became a manifestation of the living world—she became all that motivates earth to quake, air to stir, water to flow, and fire to spark. The ice gray of her eyes shifted from the color itself to the coldness of ice. The black of her hair became the black, living soil of the earth. The air around her body encircled her like a cyclone. And her hands danced with magical fire.

"Arne bought plane tickets. He's taking Maura and Akeyla to the airport this afternoon. He will not listen to reason."

"What? I thought he was going to sequester them inside The Great Hall." If they were trapped inside, at least they were *here*.

"He conferenced with the other Kings again." Her elf magic flashed, and she changed the subject. "Leave that thing here, Frank Victorsson."

I nodded. What else could I do? Dag had spoken.

I gently pulled the handle on my door before ducking out. I set the notebook down on the seat and looked at Dag for her okay. She frowned and growled, but did not tell me that it, too, needed to be left behind. I walked toward Rose's Hill and pulled up the fifth treading stone, the one at my chest level, and placed the dagger in the hollow underneath. Then I reset the stone.

I would either need to face my trials without Rose's gift, or I would need to return later to retrieve the artifact.

When I returned to the SUV, Dag had returned to her normal mundane glamour. "I want that book gone as soon as we get to your place, Frank. It's witch magic."

"Fine," I said. No use arguing with Dag. Not when her magic seethed as much as it did right now.

She glanced at me and, as if she read my mind, stopped the churning and coiling of her natural magic. It clicked and locked instead, and became the geometric, clockwork armor I'd come to expect. "You need to take them," she said. "Maura and Akeyla." She started the engine. "Take them north. Cross over into Canada and disappear into Manitoba for a couple of weeks. You need to stay with them until I can get my husband to see reason."

"The creature is my brother," I said.

Dag hit the brakes. "What?"

"He's a monster such as I, built by my father from the already-undead."

She slapped the steering wheel. "Why?" she yelled. "How?"

I shrugged. "Hubris and ingenuity."

A sour laugh hiccupped from Dag. She hit the steering wheel again. "Then perhaps it is a good thing I'm sending you into Canada, huh?"

"I take it you have not talked to Ed yet today."

She laughed again. The next string of words that fell from her lips sounded suspiciously like Icelandic profanity. "That's why you wanted to keep that... that..." She shook her head. "Listen to me, Frank Victorsson. Your family needs you. Please do not be distracted."

How was dealing with my brother a distraction from my family? "He killed one of the men who posted the video." I pointed up the tracks leading away from Rose's Hill. "He's a vampire. I need to find his daylight hiding place, use that dagger," I pointed at the hill, "and put an end to him once and for all."

She pinched the bridge of her nose. "The simplicity of vampires, huh?"

I sat back against the seat. "What does that mean?"

She gripped the steering wheel. "Arne is leaving with Maura and Akeyla in *two hours* and he's somehow convinced her that it's for the best."

I doubted that. She'd probably agreed because deep down, she was as terrified of her father as everyone else in Alfheim.

We also had a full moon coming up. "What about the wolves?" Down to The Cities and back was a full day trip.

A sour laugh popped out of Dag. "He says he'll be back in time."

"Okay, okay. Take me to The Hall. I'll see what I can do. But I need to stake my brother in the daylight. He's much too powerful in the shadows."

Dag nodded.

"Do you have your cell phone? I need to talk to Ed."

Dag stared out at the trees. Her magic swirled again, but stopped and locked down almost immediately.

She put the SUV in park. "I'll call him. You drive." She pointed at the book. "Put that in the back."

Her magic recoiled when I picked it up off my lap.

"Okay," I said, and opened my door.

I looked back at the wood dagger's resting place. It was not balanced magic, whatever it was. Or perhaps it was magic balanced on a different scale than the one used by the elves.

Either way, I couldn't shake the feeling that leaving it behind was a bad idea.

CHAPTER 23

T he sun had crested over the edge of town by the time Dag pulled the borrowed SUV into The Hall's adjacent parking lot. Gold danced over the spindly plants of the glamour surrounding the structure, and for a moment, made it look inviting.

I knew better. "Arne banned me from entering," I said.

Dag tucked her phone into her pocket. "I don't care if he told you to run naked through downtown," she said.

I chuckled. I probably shouldn't have, but Dag's posture and her tone accentuated the regality of her defiance and, to my eyes, was the most correct and satisfying occurrence of the past five days.

She chuckled, too. "You are as much a son to me as any of the men I have birthed."

I wanted to give my adoptive mother a bear hug, but I knew she would not approve. The elves, in general, were not big on public displays of affection, even hugs among family.

Except Akeyla. My niece was special.

I stepped out of the SUV. Dag hit the lock button and the vehicle chirped.

"Thanks for not driving your roadster."

Dag chuckled again. "And have you burst my leather seats? My baby must always remain pristine. You know that."

I squeezed her elbow. She accepted the contact, which, for Dag, was a major deal.

The door to the hotel burst open. Akeyla ran out, unglamoured and trailing a hot plume of fire magic.

"Grandma!" she yelled. "I don't wanna go back!"

Dag dashed across the road and snagged Akeyla into her arms just as a car rumbled by on the road. The driver didn't pay attention, and seemed more concerned about me, the huge man standing on the opposite side of the road, than the woman and child in the parking lot.

I waved, to keep his attention. He frowned, yet waved back.

When he passed, Dag had Akeyla fully glamoured again. They leaned on each other, the little girl and the matron, two females who, no matter how they worked or advanced, would always be subject to their king.

I jogged across the road. Akeyla immediately reached for me. I glanced at Dag, who nodded her okay, then scooped Akeyla up into my arms.

She buried her face in my shoulder. "I want to live with you, Uncle Frank," she said. "I can't leave Jax by himself." She looked up at my face. Tears filled her eyes and her lip quivered. "He doesn't like Ms. Saunders! He won't pay attention. What if he doesn't learn anything this year? They might hold him back and then we won't be in the same class anymore."

"Oh, honey," Dag said.

Akeyla was more concerned about Jaxson's schooling than her own banishment?

"Jax is my best friend." She sniffled.

Dag threw me a knowing look. We would have a major wolf problem on our hands if Arne separated Akeyla and Jaxson. They calmed each other, and helped each other learn. Together, they would grow into formidable leaders. Apart, they would pine and flounder. They might only be third graders, but they needed the autonomy to develop their relationship on their own terms. They also needed to learn to self-regulate without having it forced onto them.

It was the same for me. Controlling my dissociation, the hollowness, the rage—that had been a long road for me. Many people had suffered along the way, but they could not change what was me. I had to do that myself.

"I'm going to talk to your grandfather," I said.

Akeyla nodded.

"But I think we all need to go inside, okay?"

She nodded again. I hoisted her higher on my hip and walked behind Dag toward the entrance.

Maura walked out with a suitcase in each hand.

"Go back inside! Now!" Dag ordered. She reached for one of the cases, but Maura pulled it away.

Like Akeyla, she was in travel clothes, and had two knit hats in her pockets, for covering ears in case a glamour broke on the plane. Maura's eyes were swollen, and her lips and nose puffy. She'd been crying.

She set the suitcases on the ground. "Why?" she said. "What difference will it make, Mother?"

Dag's magic pulsed. Maura flinched, then hers pulsed as well. Akeyla hugged me tighter.

"I will *not* have you return to that man," Dag shouted. "I don't care what your—"

"What, Mom?" Maura yelled. "At least in Hawaii, Akeyla will be able to play outside!" She stepped to the side then back toward the suitcases. "I will not be a political pawn!"

Dag stepped back. "What?"

Maura rubbed her face. "Of course he wouldn't tell either of you." She threw her hands up in the air. "I only know because I walked in on the video call."

Did Arne mean to marry off Maura? "He can't do that, Maura," I said. "He can't—"

"Frank!" Maura pointed over her shoulder and inside the glamour around The Great Hall. "*My* grandfather decreed that if we do not leave voluntarily, then the Kings will revoke Alfheim's New Zealand colony charter."

Dag paled. "I will have my father's head," she said.

I had thought Arne and Dag as a team enough to deal with Dag's father, but Tyr Bragisson was arguably the most powerful elf on Earth. He held sway over the Norwegian and Siberian elves, and the respect of the kami in Japan. King Bragisson of the Icelandic elves controlled much of elven politics.

It had been Tyr who had given Alfheim the settlement charter for New Zealand.

Arne was just beginning to work on moving elves south. They were scouting for a colony location and establishing connections with the indigenous Maori spirits. The whole point of the colony was to make connections in the Southern Hemisphere the way the elves had with Japan after World War II. Share magic, share connections, make everyone stronger, Arne said, especially with so many mundane humans now. Magicals needed to globalize, too.

It was a massive undertaking, and the elves had chosen Arne because of all the long-lived, powerful elves, he was the only one alive who had already established a flourishing new community.

The business connections alone would be a huge economic boost for the town.

"That is the stupidest threat I have heard in a long time," I said.

Maura choked out a laugh. "This is what I was born into, Frank," she said. She pointed at her mother. "This is what Mom was born into."

Dag remained silent.

"So please, Mr. Huge-and-Strong, tell me which version of servitude is better? Controlled by my father or controlled by hers?" She reached for Akeyla. "Come, honey."

My niece sniffled and wiggled so that I would set her down.

She walked stiffly to her mother. "Why can't we live with Uncle Frank? No one will bother us if we live with Uncle Frank." She tugged on her mom's pants. "No one bothers Jax's family. And that guy at the library is a vampire." She frowned and looked up at me. "He's scary. I don't like him."

"When did Akeyla meet Tony?" I asked.

Maura shook her head. "I don't know. The school only takes the kids to the Ramsey Mansion on field trips once a year and there are always at least three elves there when they do."

"Grandpa took me. He said I was old enough to meet a vampire. He made Tony show me his fangs and how fast he could climb the wall. Grandpa said that if I ever see a vampire I should tell him or Grandma or Mom right away, even if that vampire is Mr. Biterson." She rubbed at her eyes. "Mr. Biterson didn't seem happy when Grandpa said that."

I leaned toward Maura. "We *do* have an issue right now," I said as calmly as I could muster. "One I need to deal with as soon as possible."

Maura frowned.

Dag pushed by Maura. "That's it! That elf is incorrigible. Now is not the time!"

Which elf she meant—her husband or her father—I did not know. She seemed angry enough to knock off both their heads.

"Fly off to that island if you want, daughter!" She disappeared through the glamour into Great Hall territory.

Akeyla looked between me and her mother. "Grandpa wouldn't let me say good-bye to Jax."

Both Maura and I pinched our foreheads at the same time.

"Your father is acting unexpectedly medieval," I said.

Maura snorted. A laugh followed. Akeyla looked confused, then she, too, laughed.

I knelt down to look Akeyla in the eye. "Your grandpa was right about vampires, okay? It's really important that if you sense or see one, you get away. Go to an elf or wolf you trust immediately, even if you're with Ms. Saunders."

"Or you, Uncle Frank?" She blinked a couple of times.

"Or me."

"Okay," she said.

"It's moot, Frank," Maura said. "We're leaving in less than an hour."

I stood to my full height. "No, you are not. And no, you will not be caged here, either." My sister was no one's pawn.

Maura looked more resigned than I liked. She picked up the suitcases. "We don't have any choice." She nudged her daughter. "Come on, honey. Grandpa will be out in a minute. We need to get our bags into the car."

Akeyla pulled away. "I don't want to go."

Maura sighed. "Akeyla, do as you are told."

"No!" Akeyla yelled. She stomped her little foot and a puff of fire rose off the top of her head. A small, barely perceptible puff, but a real bit of fire nonetheless.

"*This* is why we need to go," Maura said. "I have no idea how to help her with her fire magic."

No, that was not why they needed to leave. They were being forced out by men who thought only of their own power. "There are other elves who can help." There were likely Maori contacts who could teach Akeyla about her fire spirit side better than her own father.

"This is not acceptable, Maura," I said.

She closed her eyes. "What are you going to do, Frank? Get in a fistfight with Arne Odinsson, the Elf King of Alfheim, to see who has dominion over the princess?"

What? "That's not what I meant." I knew she was exasperated, but poking at me wasn't helping.

Akeyla started sobbing again. "I don't want to go!" She stomped her foot again. "I *like* living with Uncle Frank! I want to be with Jax!"

My niece ran for the glamoured entrance into The Great Hall.

"Akeyla!" Maura yelled, but her daughter had vanished behind the veil.

Maura looked at me, then at the "door." She picked up their bags and tossed them through, then ran into The Great Hall.

Should I follow? Should I let them work this out while I tracked my brother? I looked over my shoulder at the rising sun. I had an hour or two.

I ran into the glamoured world of the elves' Great Hall.

CHAPTER 24

The sun was higher inside the glamour than it was outside. Warmth spread over my neck and shoulders, and I stopped just on the other side of the door to take advantage while I listened for Maura and Akeyla.

An eagle called. Small mammals rustled. The pristine air of elf territory filled my nose with a freshness the modern world no longer had. And somewhere in here, a little elf girl ran away from her mother because her grandfather was more of a bull than a man.

I closed my eyes, cocked my head, and listened.

Nothing.

"Maura!" I called. "Akeyla!" They couldn't have gone far. The glamour distorted space and time, but not by enough for them to get so far ahead of me I could no longer see or hear their activity.

Again, nothing. No sobbing or yelling.

No chirping, either. Elf-space had suddenly gone silent.

This is bad, I thought. I had no idea why. Did Arne cause the silence? Or even more gut-clenching, did my brother?

I peered into the trees. Were the shadows darker? Were they moving? But the sun shone bright in the sky above and we were inside the glamour. Nothing should be able to get in here. *Nothing.*

The silence released and the forest around me flooded with skittering, chirping, and the lovely, sweet scent of wildflowers.

"Maura!" I called again. A few feet ahead, a large limb had fallen from one of the oaks. I snapped off a thick stick, one slightly longer than my arm, and smacked it against the limb. A loud crack echoed, but the stick held. The broken end had a bit of a point, and the blunt end a good knot.

I set it against my shoulder just in case, and headed down the path toward The Gate and The Hall.

A wild turkey tom stepped onto the path. He lifted his head, gobbled in my general direction, and made his way to the other side.

I stopped and watched him scratch at the dirt. Something was wrong. Not with the turkey per se, or the silence, or the lack of Maura and Akeyla separately. But the hairs on the back of my neck stood up. My vision clarified also, the way focus and adrenaline make colors brighter and edges sharper.

Part of me wished I hadn't listened to Dag. Part of me wished I'd brought that wood dagger with me.

"Arne?" I said. Arne could very well still be pissed enough to have added an extra anti-Frank enchantment to the glamour, and if his behavior with Maura was any indication, petty enough to do it.

Nothing but a rabbit on the trail and a huge yellow-and-black swallowtail butterfly drifting through the sunshine.

A soft, barely perceptible *click* echoed off the trees behind me.

I whipped around.

"The interesting thing about elf glamours," my brother said, "is that they change sunlight." He swung a right hook at my head.

How had he gotten so close? He was right on top of me. I ducked but his fist glanced off my ear.

I rammed the pointed end of the stick into his gut.

It went in deep, all the way to his spine. My brother growled and laughed, and swung at my head again.

I jumped back but swung for the club end of the stick, hoping to catch and brace, and hold him far enough away that he couldn't connect another jab.

153

He vanished. The stick swung with my grab and I rotated too fast, stumbled, and almost fell over. Somewhere out in the trees, the bastard laughed.

"Run, you lumbering fool," he called. Then he was right next to my side again. Right there. "Run!" he yelled in my ear.

I shifted my weight, tightened my shoulder, and hit the side of his head with my big oak stick.

My brother teetered. He gagged and stumbled, but righted himself. Slowly, he wiped blood off his ear. He showed me his hand. "We don't have that hot metallic tang mundane have."

He unsurprisingly sucked the blood off his finger.

"Should I threaten you?" He stood up straight and cracked his neck. He still wore his ash-made black suit, and his ash-made black shirt and tie. He had, somehow, culled lighter ash from his cloak and fashioned himself a pair of gray cufflinks. "Growl and huff like a *monster.*"

He winked.

I held the stick between us. "Why are you attacking Alfheim?"

He flicked the point. "I was bored. Elves are a challenge." He grinned. "You are imperfect. I am not. I'm doing Dad a favor."

Of course he was doing our father a favor. "Such a simple mind you have," I said. "So coarse and obvious. So utterly constrained by the bits from which Victor Frankenstein fashioned you."

His smugness evaporated into narrow eyes and bared fangs.

"You are as ugly as I am under that vampire glamour, aren't you?" I said. "Sallow and corpse-like? Or hunched and pathetic, like Ivan? You have no will, only your demon hunger. You are a carrion beetle."

The ash lifted off his body. It swirled and stiffened in much the same way as Dag's magic had when it formed its armor-like shell. Sigils formed. Lines and angles doubled, then tripled. Proportions oriented.

My brother's ash magic was no armor.

It was a portal—a portal Arne missed because my brother carried it on his body.

My brother, when he came through, had fashioned the portal *itself* into his cloak. Not the ash. The ash just filled it, the way it backfilled the mirage of Rose's cottage.

He grabbed the stick and yanked me into himself.

CHAPTER 25

"Do you know yourself?" my brother asked. "Do you understand from whom you are fashioned?"

Did I care? I wasn't sure that I did. It was hard to care when floating in The Land of the Dead. I'd lost my need to rip my brother's semi-beating heart from his chest.

Holding on to *any* desire to move forward—to change—seemed in itself a monumental feat.

There's an orientation to The Land of the Dead, a sense of direction, but not much else. The Land of the Dead was the end of the cul-de-sac—the empty lot at the end of a long, shadowed, dirt road. There was nothing here, no reason to be here, no purpose whatsoever beyond that this place happened to be where you ended up.

Everyone ended up here in some form or another.

No breeze moved the stale air. No dust lifted off the dry, grayish ground. Nothing grew. The sun didn't care enough to bother rising, nor did the moon. Entropy didn't care either, so nothing changed. No decay. No life working to build. No roads, paths, rocks, or landmarks of any kind. Only a dry dirt and an equally uncaring, dry, gray sky.

Yet we were not alone. One can never be alone in The Land of the Dead.

"Why does it matter?" I asked. "The dead do not care how their mortal forms are used. The men who became me are long gone." I was all that was left of most of them.

My brother squared his shoulders. "Do you know what demons are?"

He was full of questions, here in The Land of the Dead, which seemed odd. "Demons are naked hunger." Demons happened when the desire to move toward one need overcame every moderating force. "The original vampire demon had been a man, a bloodthirsty ruler, and he had carried his needs for destruction and domination into The Land of the Dead."

He'd cared enough to tighten his tornado of rage into a singular thread of energy. And that thread wove itself into the first vampiric demon.

"Hunger, yes," my brother said. "It is difficult to be hungry here, which is why we vampires leave."

He spoke his words in such a matter-of-fact way that it sucked the urgency right out of the concepts of which we spoke, as if he did not understand the magnitude of the hunger needed to make a demon.

Or The Land of the Dead's overriding lack of caring also affected my demonic brother.

He grinned and his fangs expanded downward into ridiculous sabers. My science-built brother grinned at me like a saber-toothed cat. "Allow me to ask you this question: What do you think a demon carries with it when it leaves The Land of the Dead?"

"Hunger, rage, the need to make more of itself." The basic needs of any parasite.

"Have you ever wondered *why* our father's experiments worked? Why it was that an Eighteenth Century man of letters was able to reanimate your body when modern science cannot accomplish any such similar task?"

"No," I said. I'd long suspected that my father had stumbled into some sort of magic. In all honesty, I never wanted to know. I didn't want the elves to know, or the vampires, or anyone else. I only wanted to be thankful for the life I managed to make of my bits and parts.

"All it takes is one tiny touch. One part from a corpse that died because of an infection." My brother leaned toward me. "One poor fool bitten by a carrier of a *hungry* demon."

Nothing changed about The Land of the Dead around us. My brother did not call up images of the men who became me, nor did he do the same for himself.

But I felt them. They were here, drawn to what used to be them: A terrified slave full of a blinding need to survive and protect his own. A Scottish farmer who had stopped English soldiers as they raped and pillaged his people. A Norwegian sailor who would have done anything to keep his wife and young son safe. Three soldiers, all from different armies, all doing a job they hated. A poet who would have given anything for his words to live on forever. Another man who gave his life to save an unrequited love.

They were all me and they did not quite fit together. And one of them had been *infected*.

What was I?

"Father understood with me," my brother said. "He did not believe in demons. He thought it a disease." He rubbed his hands together. "When he returned from the Arctic, he realized what must have happened, so he purposefully looked for infected corpses."

And the easiest demonic infection to find and isolate was *vampire*.

"He's here, somewhere," my brother said. "Our father. I drained him dry before ripping off his head." He shrugged. "I had not yet gained enough control to consider the joys torturing him would have brought."

My brother seemed more content with having given our father a quick death than I suspected he would have been if we had stayed in The Land of the Living.

Not even a vampire was immune to the effects of The Dead.

He scowled as if reading my mind, then grabbed my arm. "Come."

Ash burst from his torso like the tentacles of a squid and sucked me back into the portal that was him.

I HIT the standing stone of The Great Hall's Gate. All breath left my lungs. All bones in my body shuddered. Every cell screamed.

My shoulder popped out of its socket.

I howled, but managed to land on my feet.

Brother laughed and vanished into a swirl of ash only to reappear sitting on a stout limb of one of the nearby oaks. "Looks painful," he called.

He was a good twenty feet away and ten feet up in the tree. The trunk groaned, and the limb dipped under his bulk, but he stayed up there, a giant gorilla of vampiric disdain.

I leaned against The Gate's massive granite side. Pain throbbed outward from the dislocation as a smothering bubble of suffocating agony. Breathing hurt. My perception contracted and pulsed with each throb. Another injury to my leg also throbbed, but I couldn't pinpoint it, not with my shoulder masking my senses.

He'd brought us back inside the elves' glamour.

Brother could move wherever he wanted. He could do whatever he pleased, to whomever he dared.

He jumped to crouching on the limb like a massive raven. "When I woke, I did not understand any more than you did," he said. "But I understood the hunger. I understood the need to control." A small plume of ash rose off his hand. "Father paid first." He pointed at me. "And now that you have let me in, I will control you. I will control these elves and their magic." He licked his lips. "The blood of an elf is... magical." He snickered at his own joke.

What could I do? How could I stop this creature?

Lure him to the dagger, or lure him back into The Land of the Dead and somehow make his stay permanent?

"Oh!" He twirled his finger through the air. "You're considering ways to hold me in The Land of the Dead! You would not make a good poker player, my brother."

I leaned my head against the stone and scowled up at the tree.

He laughed again. "I've walked this Earth as me almost as long as you have walked as you. Do you honestly think ridding your world of me will be—"

The head of a magical arrow pierced his heart and breastbone, and appeared as a shimmering silver point in the center of his chest.

Brother coughed. He looked down at the arrow, then vanished.

The arrow and its shaft clinked off the tree limb and bounced to the ground.

"Stay hidden!" I yelled. The archer might not be Dag. Several other elves were skilled enough to take on my vampiric brother. Another elf, though, would be in much greater danger than the Queen of Alfheim.

Brother appeared directly in front of me and landed a right jab into my face.

He vanished again.

Another arrow flew by my arm.

Brother reappeared to my side and plucked the arrow from the air. He twisted.

The arrow drove into the deltoid of my damaged shoulder. I howled again and dropped to my knees.

Brother raised his arms. "I will kill all of you!" he yelled. "One by one. I will not stop. I will not pause. I will cleanse this town of elves and wolves." He kicked my side. "And pathetic first draft—"

The battle axe almost did its job. It almost took off his head, but he vanished again.

"Get up," Maura said. She groaned and hoisted the huge, silver axe onto her shoulder.

The object was covered with sigils and runes, many of which glowed with magic. The shaft also glimmered as if made from a branch of a magical tree.

The axe had obviously been made for someone much larger than Maura. "Give me that." I held out my good arm. "I can swing it faster."

"Elf made. Elf wielded," she said. "With two good arms."

I needed a weapon. "You need to run," I said. "Take whoever is shooting arrows and get to The Hall." I extended my hand again. "Please."

Magic streamed off Maura's eyes. It jumped and danced through her hair, but it had not condensed around her the way her mother's had condensed into armor.

Maura was vulnerable.

"You're wounded. You need us," she said. "I *will not* allow that thing to—"

Brother punched Maura in the face, then vanished again.

She gulped, her hand coming up to her now-broken nose, and stumbled into the granite of The Gate.

Brother appeared again, this time out of hand-to-hand distance. "The tastiest elves? The littlest ones."

He vanished again.

All the color drained from Maura's face and magic. She gulped again.

Another punch sent her head ricocheting off the granite.

He appeared between us. "I will rip that child into pieces. Then I will rip apart her wolf-born proto-mate." He walked two of his fingers across his palm. "And then the elves can build themselves a mini version of you and me."

My brother vanished one final time.

CHAPTER 26

"Akeyla!" Maura wheezed. She buckled forward. "What did he do to me?"

Her magic crackled. It fractured much like it had when she and Akeyla returned from Hawaii—bruised patches appeared.

I slammed my shoulder against the rock and popped it back into its socket. The agony lapped itself in my cycle of pain and turned into screeching, screaming, white-hot needles. Nausea welled up, but I somehow managed to hold it in check.

I needed to kill my brother.

"Where's Akeyla?" I asked. "Please tell me she's with Arne."

Arne could hold his own against any vampire. Or so I hoped.

Maura nodded. "Dad took her when he left." She held her hand against her nose and muttered more Icelandic swear words. "We saw that monster take you," she gasped. "Mom and I." She looked up at me and waved her free hand. "Dad had to go to the wolves. He needed to make sure they knew what was happening. It's moonrise."

Moonrise? "It's mid-morning."

Maura shook her head. "You've been gone for *hours*, Frank. It's night." She coughed again. "At least Dad realized that tossing us onto that damned plane was not a smart choice right now."

My brother had me in The Land of the Dead for hours? "It had only been moments," I said.

"Why am I not healing?" She pressed on her nose again.

The elves healed quickly. Maura had healed from the fire at Lara's Café within a day or two. A broken nose would take as long, but she should have stopped bleeding by now.

My shoulder screamed when I reached for her. I wasn't healing, either.

Dag staggered out of the trees holding her arm unnaturally against her side. Her shattered bow hung from her belt.

Her magic was just as bruised as her daughter's—and someone had broken her elbow.

"Mom!" Maura stumbled to her mother.

A bolt of power jolted up my arm the moment I tried to pick up Maura's axe—a bolt much like the one I'd felt when I picked up the dagger. "You two need medical attention." I pulled back my hand. "Whatever he's doing, it's affecting your magic."

Dag leaned against the rock and nodded, but didn't speak.

I tried to pick up the axe again, and again, it zapped me. "Why can't I pick up the axe?"

"Elf made," Maura said again. "Elf wielded."

Dag closed her eyes and lifted her undamaged hand off her broken elbow. She drew a circle in the air, then lines. A sigil formed. "Place your hands inside the ring," she said.

I stuck both my hands through the magic.

I felt nothing unusual. No tingling or numbness. But the magic collapsed around my hands like a pair of gloves.

"The axe will now think you're an elf," Dag said. "It won't last long so use it wisely."

"How long?" I asked. *Won't last long* could mean half an hour or half a year, with elves.

Dag slid down the side of the rock. "Morning."

Either myself or my brother would be dead by sunrise, then. "Is there anything I need to know?" I asked. "The axe isn't going to turn into a cloud of pixies if I take it out into the moonlight, is it?"

Dag closed her eyes and leaned against the rock. "Its purpose is to damage, Frank, not entertain."

"Good." I swung it with my good arm, to get a feel for its weight. I could definitely take off my brother's head with this particular weapon.

"I need the keys to the SUV and a phone," I said. "Arne better talk to me."

"He will." Dag's voice suggested there'd been an argument. Maura's expression confirmed my suspicion. "The keys and my phone are in my quiver."

She leaned forward so I could pull the items from the small pocket at the base.

"Get help," I said. I didn't like how Maura continued to bleed. "And get somewhere safe."

Dag grunted. "We are in the safest place in Alfheim. I do not believe it will do us any good to run away."

She drew a small circle on the side of Maura's nose. The bleeding slowed. Dag looked up at me. "Be careful, my adopted son. Be vigilant. And do what you must."

I bowed my head. "Thank you," I said. "I will."

I ran for the exit to the real world.

I HIT the key fob as I staggered into the parking lot. The SUV *whooped* and the lights flashed—at least Brother hadn't thought to trash all the vehicles in the lot.

I had the axe. Was returning to Rose's Hill for the dagger a waste of time? Arne might know. I dialed Dag's phone as I started the SUV.

Arne answered. "Where the hell have you been?" he said.

"Me or your wife, Odinsson?" I answered. "Tell me you have Akeyla with you."

"I do." Arne paused. "Speak."

I pulled the SUV out onto the road and headed in the general direction of Rose's Hill and the open forest Gerard said the wolves would run this full moon. "The vampire is my brother."

No discernable noise crossed the connection. For a second, I wondered if he'd hung up.

"How is such a thing possible?" he asked.

"Arne, he threatened to come after Akeyla." It was already night. Brother could move around Alfheim without restriction. "He hurt Maura and Dag. I told them to get medical attention."

I put the phone on speaker and dropped it into the cup holder so I could keep my hands on the steering wheel, even if my damaged arm continued to throb.

"How badly? You left my wife and daughter unprotected?"

I rubbed my face. What to say? Arne needed to keep his wits about him—and to make sure he stayed with his granddaughter.

But he also needed to stay with the wolves. The last thing Alfheim needed was for Brother to thrall one of the new wolves. A thralled wolf might lose control and rip apart a mundane—which would cause even more chaos on which my brother could feed.

Arne's old ways of thinking about the women were not helping.

"By Odin's plucked-out eyeball, you are one rightful bastard, aren't you?" I grumbled.

"What did you say, Frank?" he grumbled back.

I turned onto the main road and increased the SUV's speed. "*I need to stop my brother. You need to protect Akeyla. Dag and Maura are fine but they cannot help because they need medical attention.*" Arne did not take well to direct orders. Not from me. Not from his wife. And certainly not from the other Kings.

Yet he'd rolled his daughter and granddaughter under that bus.

"Maura and Akeyla cannot go back to Hawaii. No elf should force them to go, no matter the politics. This is not Medieval Norway." Nor was it the continental European time in which my father sewed me together—or the time in which he so stupidly reconstructed a vampire.

A vampire who could move in and out of The Land of the Dead.

One more vicious than any vampire I'd ever dealt with in the past. One primal and demonic, yet worldly.

"He wants to destroy the elves," I said. "Don't fall into his traps."

"Akeyla is safe." That's all Arne said. Nothing else. No response to my other words. Only *Akeyla is safe.*

Which made me think that she was not. "Where is she?"

"With me. With the wolves."

Who were about to take their wolf forms for the night. "How is that safe?" Running with the wolves was complicated. A lot went into the preparation, and though Akeyla often waited in The Great Hall, Arne had not yet allowed her out in the woods with twenty-odd were-wolves, some of whom were still novices.

"This is our best option."

Perhaps he was correct. Perhaps the threat of the wolves would be enough to keep Brother away from Akeyla.

Or perhaps he'd use the chaos to flicker in and snatch her away.

"My brother pulled me into The Land of the Dead," I said. "He can move in and out at will. He could appear any place at any second."

I let the fact sink in that Arne's brazen use of his magic to destroy any possible portal had not worked.

"Ed said he has an aversion to light," Arne said.

"Yes," I said. "Though he appeared inside The Hall's enchantment during daylight."

Arne swore. "He's using in-place enchantments to filter?" He swore again. "We are not dealing with a normal vampire."

I turned off the main road onto the lane that would take me to the trail up to Rose's Hill. "No, he is not." Any more than I was a normal man.

"And you say he is your... brother? How is that possible?"

"He showed me. I'll explain once we have this situation under control."

"This situation is already out of hand," Arne responded. "It's bigger than Akeyla. It involves all of Alfheim." He paused again. "First the video. Now your neighbors claim they have video of you murdering a man on their beach."

My stomach jumped. I'd forgotten about the neighbors. "Does Ed have them under control?" If they had video, it might not show what they think it did. "They were thralled," I said.

"That's what Ed said. He impounded their phones, but they're lawyers. They're causing a stink." Arne sounded as if he rubbed his forehead.

Of course they were. "My brother probably picked them specifically because he understood the level of impact they could make," I said. "He seems well-versed on how to manipulate modern mundanes."

Arne *humphed*. "Can you draw him out?"

I didn't know. I'd never tried. "I hope so," I said. "I have a weapon." I glanced at the elven "gloves" on my hands. "I'm picking up another. Where should I meet you?"

A low howl echoed across the connection.

I looked out the windshield at the bright, round moon.

The first wolves were changing.

"Akeyla!" Arne yelled. "Come here!" Noise rustled.

"Uncle Frank?" she said. "Grandpa says we don't have to go right away and I get to be with Jax when he changes."

She sounded more excited than she should have, and I wondered what Arne had told her about why she got to stay with her friend.

"That's good, honey," I said. "Promise me you will stay right next to your grandfather, okay? I mean right with him. He needs your help."

"But he's mean, Uncle Frank."

Whatever he'd said hadn't calmed her anger. "Well, yes he is, but that doesn't mean you shouldn't help him tonight."

"He goes out with the wolves every full moon," she said. "He was going to drop us at the airport and drive back to be with the wolves because he does this all the time."

"Tonight's special," I said. "Okay?"

"Do you need my help, Grandpa?" she asked.

"I do, Akeyla," Arne said in the background.

"If you send me back I will *never* help you again," she said.

I held in a laugh. Leave it to Akeyla to put Arne Odinsson in his place.

"Akeyla!" he snapped.

"I second the kid, Arne," I said. Best not to threaten the Elf King of Alfheim, but sometimes the man needed to understand how his actions affected others.

"Where are you headed?" Arne was changing the subject.

"Rose's Hill," I said.

"Call again when you are ready to meet us."

He hung up.

I turned onto the trail toward a wooden dagger I hoped was the magic I needed to end the horror that was my brother.

CHAPTER 27

I checked the SUV glove compartment for a flashlight, then checked the back for a toolbox. I found nothing useful, which left me with the phone's light.

The battery sat at about half. I'd need to be careful. Calls out were just as important as seeing where I stepped. With the full moon, I'd be able to see. But without a bright, direct source of light, my brother could appear at any time.

Or in any place.

I left the SUV running and the headlights glaring, and walked toward the step where I'd hidden the dagger.

Dag had seemed upset by it, but I hadn't seen any anti-elf magic. But then again, I saw no magic around Brother, either.

Perhaps the dagger was as cloaked as he was.

I lifted off the stone. The dagger waited right where I'd left it. I reached to pick it up… and I couldn't. I couldn't touch it.

The gloves wouldn't let me.

I looked at my hands. "Could you, this once?" I asked.

The magic around my palms clicked and twirled. I tried again to pick up the dagger, and again, I couldn't lift it.

The gloves *whirled* as if they were actual machinery. Soft blues and greens lifted off my skin and the magic of the gloves took on a reddish glow. This time I got the sense that I'd be able to lift the dagger.

It released from the soil with an audible *pop*. I flipped it over. The underside looked the same. No marks, and the center shaft of liquid looked undamaged.

"What are you?" I asked it. The blade, of course, did not answer. I looked over my shoulder. Would the axe react the same way as the gloves? Dag's responses suggested it might not be a good idea to set them next to each other.

"I hope it was worth retrieving you," I said. I walked back toward the SUV and wrapped the dagger in a towel I'd found in the back, then set it down next to the axe.

They moved apart as if pushed by magnets.

I reached for the axe… and couldn't pick it up.

"This is not good," I said to the gloves. The magic had responded to my voice; maybe it would this time, too. "Can you turn blue again?"

The gloves whirred. Sigils lifted. And they changed back to blue—except this time, a slight purple haze hung around the magic's lines and curves.

I picked up the axe and swung it left, then right, checking its balance one more time. My shoulder continued to throb, but mobility had returned, so if needed, I could attack from either side. The axe balanced well, and slid through the air with an ease only an elf-made weapon had.

I set it down and pulled out Dag's phone.

"Meet us at your place," Arne said, and hung up.

Our last conversation must have taken all the talk out of Arne Odinsson. I closed the rear of the SUV and made my way to the driver's seat. From here, I'd need to drive by the lawyers' chrome monstrosity.

I turned the SUV around and made my way toward the lake.

No call from Arne saying that my brother had appeared and

attempted to snatch Akeyla. No attempt to attack me, either. I was beginning to wonder if wandering in and out of The Land of the Dead took an energy toll.

And if so, how could I use it to my advantage?

Thing was, I couldn't see Brother's magic. I couldn't sense him. I didn't have enough information about his powers to understand how he did what he did, much less how to utilize any vulnerabilities.

"I was bored" did not give me a true motivation for his attacks, nor did "elves provide a challenge." And why would he wait over a century before coming for me if my presence on this Earth angered him so?

Either he had not known of my existence, or up until recently, he hadn't cared.

Or perhaps his sense of time was distorted. What seemed like moments in The Land of the Dead were much longer in reality.

I doubted I would know, and not knowing the details of an enemy added a fog to planning. I would rather not take that chance.

Perhaps I would get lucky. Perhaps the dagger in his heart and the elf blade taking off his head would put an end to my brother and all his bits.

I slowed as I approached the road around the lake. To the left, my house. To the right, the lawyers' chrome behemoth. Directly ahead, a small break in the trees that allowed me to see the still water.

I'd be home in about five minutes; perhaps Arne had an understanding I lacked. I just hoped he would listen to reason.

The SUV bounced over a pothole. The headlights dipped for a split second.

Brother appeared directly in front of the vehicle.

I slammed on the brakes. The SUV corkscrewed around the pothole—one front tire dropped into the hole while all the others slid.

Brother pushed.

I *felt* the wave of magic. No color changes. No visual signs. Just a pressure wave on my eardrums lowering the pitch of the world, plus a thrust back and to the side.

The SUV flipped as if I'd hit that pothole at sixty miles an hour.

The vehicle tumbled over. What had been up became down and

what had been down became up. My head swayed and my hands came off the steering wheel. Then up became up again and the SUV slammed into a massive pine.

My protection spells ballooned outward like magical airbags.

The pine's trunk cracked against the rear passenger side door. The SUV cracked right along with it, and if I hadn't had on my seatbelt, I would have cracked against the windshield, spells or not.

In the back, a whine rose from the tumbling axe and dagger.

I knew what was about to happen. I don't know how, but I understood that the blast about to come from the back of the SUV would be significantly worse than Brother throwing the vehicle at a tree.

"Wait until he gets close!" I yelled and unbuckled my seatbelt. The door wouldn't open. I kicked, and it budged. I kicked again.

The whine grew in pitch.

The door flew open. Brother reached in and grabbed me around the neck. "You and I have—"

The bolt of full-spectrum magic that exploded off the touching axe and dagger filled the entire area with a blindingly bright flash.

My brother screamed. He dropped his hold and staggered away from the SUV.

The scar on his cheek and neck glowed like a lightning bolt. Light flooded up behind his ear and into his black hair. It flowed down his neck and glowed brightly enough that I saw it through his suit of ash.

My brother, the monster built of vampire parts, roared.

He dropped to his knees. "I was going to torture her," he growled. "I was going to suck her and all the other miserable citizens of this pathetic little backwater dry in front of you and your pitiable need for love and family."

He touched his chest as the magic from his bolt-scar faded. "But now I think I'll just snap her neck."

He vanished.

"No, no, no…" I patted my pockets. No phone.

It was in the SUV. I scrambled back and crawled in, patting at the seats and the floor before finding the phone under the passenger seat.

"Arne!" I yelled when he answered. "He just flipped my SUV. He's coming for Akeyla. He'll snatch her. Keep her close!"

In the background, Akeyla screamed.

And directly ahead, across the road and through the small break in the trees, a shadow—a hole in the world—ran across the water toward the Carlson house.

CHAPTER 28

The dagger, once again, would not allow me to pick it up. I grabbed the towel and tried with the fabric between the dagger and my hand; this time, I could hold it long enough to wrap it and place it in my waistband.

The axe also seemed to be tired and cranky, but it allowed me to hold onto its handle and walk with it, as long as I carried it on the shoulder opposite the dagger.

"What did you two do?" I asked, not expecting an answer.

I got one. Not a spoken one, but I knew in the same way I had known they were about to flash magic: They were not compatible, but they agreed on their purpose. That agreement allowed them to channel their incompatibility into a shared action.

The axe and the dagger had a full-fledged "the enemy of my enemy is my friend" truce happening. But I was also never to touch them together again. The truce only went so far.

"I'm glad you two came to an understanding," I said, as I jogged onto the road. Both of my shoulders ached now, as did my right leg, but nothing was broken, and I could move.

I ran toward the Carlson house.

I had no idea if Brother had hurt Arne. After Akeyla screamed, the connection died. But I'd yet to see him or his car.

My focus needed to be Akeyla. I'd worry about Arne later.

I rounded the bend into the driveway and parking area on the land side of the Carlson house. A huge dumpster sat off to the side in front of a stand-alone three-car garage. The moon hit the smaller building's metal siding and the entire gravel parking area in front of the house glowed with a harsh, blue light.

They were here. They had to be. The silence around the building was as eerie as the reflected moonlight and meant only one thing—a vampire.

The axe vibrated, and for a second my body reacted as if I had my cell phone on my shoulder. I looked up at the blade.

Magic whipped around the head of the axe like a hive of angry pixies. Blues mingled with reds and purples. Greens burst from churning sigils. Pale yellows flickered.

"I take it you've recharged?" I asked.

It hadn't so much recharged as become pissed off. On my belt, on the other side, the dagger didn't do anything other than be.

Where the axe felt alive, the dagger was more of an object, a thing made from something that used to be alive.

"I'm going to have to use the dagger," I said.

The axe knew. And, somehow, promised to change my gloves when the moment arrived.

But it would be the last time. Once the switch happened, there would be no switching back.

"Let's hope an elf shows up to help, then, huh?" I said.

The axe agreed.

I closed my eyes and listened. Something shuffled on the beach. And someone gagged.

I ran around the house. No reason to be subtle or to think I would surprise Brother.

My boots hit a softer area on the beach pebbles. I skidded around the corner of the house and out into the blasting glow of the full moon.

Yellow and black police tape crisscrossed between his shadowy body and where I stopped fifteen feet away. He stood on the beach in the exact spot where he'd killed the man who'd taken the video of Akeyla.

She stood in front of Brother, her hands clasped to the chest of her pale pink hoodie and her eyes and face equally pale from terror. "Uncle Frank," she said.

Brother grinned and lifted his hand to set it on her shoulder.

I may lumber, but I am fast. I whipped the axe at his head.

Akeyla screamed and, thankfully, ducked. She immediately bolted under the police tape and ran up the beach toward me.

Brother twisted. The axe flew by his head and directly into pallet of siding. He twisted back and reached over the tape for Akeyla.

He snagged her by the hood. She screamed again. I ran forward fully intending to tackle him to the ground.

Akeyla's hood ignited. Flames leaped from the fabric to my brother's hand and he snatched back his fingers.

"You little brat!" He swung his fist at her head.

I hit him at a full run and we tumbled across the beach toward the pallet and the axe. The police tape wrapped around us as we rolled and punched, but it didn't seem to be hindering my brother's hits.

He slammed my shoulder into the ground. "What's more delicious? You watching me drain her, or her watching me drain you?"

His fangs appeared. Brother raised his head to bite into my neck.

The protection spell along the side of my head kicked him in the teeth. His head snapped back and he rolled off me.

Akeyla slapped at her hood but stood her ground. "Leave Uncle Frank alone!" she yelled, and slapped at her hood again.

Brother jumped to a squat and wiped blood off his lip, then swatted at the police tape still coiled around his legs. "I can dislocate your shoulder but the spells won't allow me to break your skin?" he said. "Fascinating."

The shadows around Brother deepened. He was about to jump into The Land of the Dead.

I shot up and reached for the axe.

The police tape around Brother's legs ignited.

"Yes!" yelled Akeyla. "Go away!"

Brother howled and slapped at the flames. The shadows tightened. He vanished.

"Akeyla!" I yelled as I pulled the axe from the pallet. "Come here, honey!" He couldn't snatch her if she was right next to me.

She ran down the beach.

Brother appeared directly between us. Directly in front of the running Akeyla. She screamed and did her best not to skid on the pebbles but I knew she wouldn't be able to stop. He'd have her again.

I lifted the axe to swing, but it refused to leave my hand. "What..." I said.

A small black-and-violet canine body leaped from the top of the pallet.

"Jaxson!" I yelled. "Down!" If I got the axe in the right place, I could take off my brother's head.

Jax latched onto Brother's ear and shook his head.

Brother swatted at the young wolf but Jax was too fast. He landed between the monster and Akeyla, Brother's ripped-off ear in his mouth.

Jax spit out the ear and growled loudly.

My brother touched the side of his head. "Well, well," he said, and slowly picked up the ear. He looked at it, then placed it back where it belonged.

I could not reassemble myself. Not like that.

Brother grinned. "Guess I'll kill them both." He snatched for Jax.

The kid snapped at his hand and danced out of the way.

"Leave Jax alone!" Akeyla yelled. A bit of stray construction timber on the shore caught fire.

Brother looked down at the wood, then at Akeyla, then over his shoulder at me. "She's as much of a monster as you and I."

If I threw the axe, he'd dodge again. The axe agreed.

"Put that axe down, dear brother," he said. "Set it on the pebbles and step away from it." He rolled his shoulders. "It won't kill me, but that damned thing does hurt." He chuckled. "I kind of like it."

Jax inched around so he was between Brother and Akeyla. I nodded toward the house, hoping that the kids would understand.

My brother, thankfully, ignored me.

I set the axe on the ground. "You need to go red now," I whispered, hoping the gloves and the axe were listening.

"Oh, I started red, dear brother." He sniffed and made of show of looking bored.

Behind him, Jax nuzzled Akeyla and she turned to run for the house.

My brother blinked. He snarled and stepped toward the kids.

The magic around my hands lifted off. Sigils cycled. The mechanics of compatibility switched from elf to whatever made the dagger, and I reached for the towel in my waistband.

I threw the dagger at my brother's heart.

He twisted again, but not fast enough. The dagger lodged in his shoulder.

"Go!" I yelled. Akeyla and Jax ran for the house.

My brother howled. The magical bolt-scar on his neck and shoulder brightened again. All his muscles tensed and he dropped to all fours.

He tried to grab the hilt. He tried to pull it out, but like me, he couldn't touch it.

The magic of the dagger would not allow him to remove it—but it hadn't killed him, either.

He roared again. His ash tightened around his body but the bolt-scar flared and it dissipated.

I kicked him in the head.

He grabbed for my leg but I dropped my knee and swung my fist down toward the dagger.

It wouldn't allow me to touch it, either. I couldn't pull it out. I couldn't push it in. It had lodged next to his collarbone with only the hilt sticking out and no one was going to move it.

Brother grinned yet again. "Looks like we are at an impasse." He pushed me down and ran for the house and the kids.

Akeyla and Jax wiggled between two beams and disappeared into the building. Brother pulled up short. Neither he nor I could wiggle through anything and unless he figured out how to vanish with the dagger in his shoulder, they were safe.

"Will you let me pick up the axe again?" I asked the gloves.

No, they couldn't. Not without a recharge from an elf.

I'd have to kill my brother with my bare hands. What killed vampires? Sunlight. Stakes in the heart. Beheading. Fire. The moon was high, but he didn't like any direct source of light. I pulled Dag's phone out of my pocket and turned on the light.

He howled and shaded his eyes. His hand came down on the temporary door's lock. The metal groaned, then snapped.

He whipped the lock at me.

I ducked but he was through the entrance and into the house before I could pull him away.

The phone's light blasted a bright tunnel through the lower-level shadows as I followed him inside. The kids had a lot of piles of debris to hide behind, but the house was as open and shiny inside as it was outside and offered few nooks in which they could hide.

"Out the front!" I yelled. "Both of you! Go!" They needed to get out.

No sounds of them scurrying. No sounds of Brother, either.

Jax howled, then yipped.

I swung around a short wall into a narrow hallway that ran from the lake side of the house toward what looked like a set of bedrooms. Dust swirled in the air, and shuffling echoed off the bare sheetrock.

I checked the first bedroom. Nothing. Same for the second. I held out my light and checked the third.

My brother stood in the middle of the room. Jax lay on the floor, thankfully huffing, with Brother's foot on his neck. Brother held Akeyla by the arm.

"Turn off that light," he snarled and shook Akeyla to make his point.

I turned off the light.

Brother straightened. "Which one first, dear Frank? The boy?" He pressed down on Jax's neck. "Or our little fire starter?" He looked down at Akeyla.

I threw the phone. It bounced off his temple.

Brother staggered just enough to allow Jax to get away, but Akeyla yelped as he grabbed her by the neck.

"Jax! Go! Get your parents. Now!" I yelled.

The kid rolled to his feet. He yipped and looked up at Akeyla. "Go!" she said.

He dipped his head and ran out of the room.

"What is a pack of werewolves going to do?" Brother lifted Akeyla into the air so they were eye to eye. "Parts of me have dealt with werewolves. Parts of me have dealt with elves."

"Let her go," I said. He wouldn't listen. His anger was as focused on the elves as it was on me, but I had to try.

"You are such a tiny thing," he said to my niece.

Akeyla kicked. Her little foot came up and she kicked him in the shoulder.

She hit the dagger.

He gasped. She dropped the four feet to the ground as he tried to swat at the wood he still could not touch.

Akeyla hit the floor hard. Her leg crumpled and her head bounced off the concrete. She yipped much like Jax had, then groaned.

Brother's foot pulled back. He was going to kick.

He'd kill her. A kick to her gut would do enough damage that no elf's healing spells could save her.

I dropped my shoulder and ran directly into his side. Breath left us both, as did our footing, and we fell against the bare framing of the room's inner wall.

"I will rip you down to your component parts," my brother snarled. "I will dissemble your body and I will destroy your soul. I will feast on—"

The dagger hilt—the red-stained bit of wood sticking out of his shoulder—caught fire.

I let go. Brother swatted at the dagger but still couldn't touch it. Couldn't stop the flames. I scrambled back.

His face changed. Not his strong-jawed features, but the way he held the muscles underneath. "Where am I?" He blinked, and his expression changed again—as did his accent. "Oh, mate...."

Was my brother disassembling?

The wall framing around him burst into flames. He yelped and swung his arms.

I scrambled toward Akeyla. "Honey..." I said. "No more fire, okay?"

"What, Uncle Frank?" she said. The wall on the other side also ignited.

The wood crackled. Smoke wicked from the framing. The paper on the wall board at the back of the room lit, and dust puffed into the room.

The house burned. Heat rose. My brother coughed. The dagger smoked, though it no longer burned, but whatever Akeyla did still affected his mind. He looked down at Akeyla, then at me. "Who are you?" Then he ran from the room.

I gently picked up Akeyla. I had to get her out of the house. I had to get *me* out of the house. But all the walls burned. All of them. Flame sputtered and heat singed my eyes and...

The rage wanted to surface. It bubbled up from deep in my gut, from a shadow place like my brother's portal into The Land of the Dead. The terror and the agony and the blame. Was I paralyzed? Was I flailing? How could I be both?

If I didn't move, Akeyla would die in here.

She coughed and curled her arms around my neck. "I'm sorry, Uncle Frank," she said.

I patted at the protection enchantments on my scalp. "Come on," I said. "Please."

They expanded around us, but the fire wasn't magic. It was real flame in a real house. The enchantments offered some protection from the smoke, but not the heat.

In the great room, down the hall and between us and the lake-side exit from the house, a beam shattered. The *crack* of the rupture reverberated through the entire house. The floor shook.

We were trapped. I hadn't moved fast enough. I hadn't pulled my little niece to my chest and run through the flames to safety.

But I wouldn't rage. I couldn't. Not if there was some chance I could save Akeyla.

"I can't breathe," she said.

"Can you make an enchantment?" I said. "Something that gets you air?" Maybe she could save herself. "Don't worry about me, honey, okay? You breathe."

"I didn't start that fire in the café," she said.

"I know," I said. "The man who attacked us did."

She held on as best she could. "My head hurts."

I dropped down to the floor and tucked her as close as possible to keep us below the smoke. "Please honey. Stay—"

A tongue of magic poked through the flames. It curled outward and touched Akeyla, then flicked over me. Then it disappeared back toward the lake.

Elves. Someone had come.

"We're back here!" I yelled. The fire roared and the smoke choked, but someone might hear us.

A wave of magic burst through the flames. Ice blues danced before us. Greens swirled. Purples shifted and slid and pushed back the smoke. The air cooled.

My protection spells reached out and a tunnel opened through the fire.

I lifted Akeyla and pushed off the floor. I would not look at the flames. I would ignore the heat and the soot. I would not be deterred.

I hopped the downed beam and carried Akeyla out the broken door onto the lakeshore.

And right into a mundane recording his burning house.

CHAPTER 29

"What are you people?" Aaron Carlson yelled. He waved his phone. "Who was that huge guy in black who ran out?" He pointed at me. "Did you do this?"

I took in the shore. Dag stood by the water, her arms out and her magic holding back the flames. Maura ran toward us. Both elves still maintained their glamours, but were obviously engaged in an activity Carlson did not understand.

"Akeyla!" Maura reached for her daughter.

Her nose and face were swollen, but she wasn't bleeding anymore. Dag looked ghostly white. Moving her broken elbow to perform the magic needed to open the tunnel must have caused a level of agony that would have dropped a lesser elf.

And she'd done it in front of a mundane holding a camera.

I handed Akeyla to her mother. "I think she has a concussion." Then I grabbed for Aaron Carlson's phone. "Give me that."

He danced out of the way. "Why?" He continued to hold up the phone. "My wife saw you kill that man!"

"A vampire thralled her to see what he wanted her to see!" I roared.

He blinked. His mouth rounded. "You are *crazy!*" he said.

Maura carried Akeyla toward her mother. "They're out, Mom! You can stop."

Behind me, the tunnel collapsed. Dag dropped to her knees on the edge of the lake.

Aaron Carlson gasped. "How are you doing that?" He pointed at me. "What are you?" he asked again.

Jaxson bounded out of the shadows toward Maura and Akeyla.

Aaron Carlson pointed. "That's a wolf!"

A huge silver-and-black dire-wolf-like werewolf and a graceful blue-black smaller wolf followed Jax out of the shadows. Gerard and Axlam had heard their son's calls and must have brought Dag and Maura.

"Oh my God," Carlson breathed.

Three more adult werewolves followed.

I grabbed him by the collar and hauled him away from his burning house. "They're the Alfheim Pack," I said. "They don't take kindly to mundanes threatening their children."

Jaxson nuzzled Akeyla.

"Jax," she said, and hugged him. "I knew you'd get help."

Off in the distance, sirens blared. Fire and Safety would be here in moments.

"Where's Arne?" I asked. Did Brother hurt the King of Alfheim so badly he couldn't step up for his people?

"Arne Odinsson? The mayor's husband?" Carlson pointed at Dag. "Her arm is broken but she did *something*. I'm going to—"

"If you release any video, if you tell anyone about any of this, I will rip off your head," I growled. I didn't murder. I wouldn't murder. But that didn't mean I couldn't intimidate.

Aaron Carlson stepped back. "Are you threatening me, Mr. Victor—?"

Magic appeared around his head. He gasped, and froze in place.

The shadows parted. Arne Odinsson hobbled out of the trees, Remy at his side, and made his way toward his wife.

He leaned against Remy. He'd bled a lot from a wound on his leg, which I suspected made him more ornery than woozy. But like Dag and Maura, he still maintained his glamour. "You used magic in front of a mundane with a camera?"

Dag pushed herself to standing. "He was already here when we arrived. Neither Maura nor I were in any shape to silence him or send him away."

"You repeated the mistakes of earlier?" Arne said.

He'd have to send away his wife now, too. And the wolves. And me. There was no other choice.

Arne wasn't any more likely to kill Aaron Carlson than I was.

He walked toward us and plucked Aaron Carlson's phone from his frozen hand. "Did you upload any video?"

Carlson tried to speak. Arne frowned and waved his hand. Some of the magic around the mundane's head loosened.

"We have an automatic security system. I turned it on after what happened last night. That's why I came out here."

Arne looked up at the burning house. The lights of the fire truck were visible now along the road. He pointed at the woods. "Take the women and the pack and stay in the trees," he said to Remy. "When the EMTs arrive, make sure they get help."

The big wolf nodded, then lifted his head and howled. The pack quickly surrounded Dag, Maura, and Akeyla, and led them toward cover.

Arne extended his hand toward me. I offered my arm. He nodded once and steadied himself. "Do I kill him?" he asked.

Carlson gasped.

"I don't know if that will help, Arne," I said.

"You have no idea how many people you will hurt if you tell the wider world about us," Arne said to the mundane. "Akeyla. Maura. Jax and his family. Half my town. Frank here. Nor do you understand the threats from which we protect you and your kind."

"That man you saw running from the house? He's a vampire," I said. "A *powerful* vampire who is as likely to find you in The Cities as he is here." I pointed at the burning house. "Without our protection, he will eat your family."

I lied. Arne knew it, but Aaron Carlson did not.

185

The truth was I had no idea at all if Brother would attack the Carlsons. I had no idea if he would attack the elves or the wolves or me again. He had seemed different, when he ran away. Smaller. Less violent.

The dagger may not have killed him, but it seemed to have diminished his power.

Arne closed his eyes. "I'm tired, Frank."

The heat of the fire prickled my back and I, too, wanted to close my eyes. Maybe we'd all wake up tomorrow in a better, calmer place.

"What are you?" Carlson asked yet again.

Arne looked at me, then he looked out over the lake.

He dropped his glamour. His ears manifested, followed closely by his lynx-like sideburns and his massive, swaying, silver-clasped ponytail. His leathers appeared next, and his elven shimmer.

Carlson gasped yet again.

"Elves, Mr. Carlson," he said. He leaned closer. "I sailed to this land with your Norse ancestors."

Carlson looked at me.

"I'm a *jotunn*," I said. "A giant."

Arne laughed. "That you are, my son. That you are." He re-glamoured just as the trucks pulled up on the road side of the house.

"You're *elves*? Like magic and fairies and trolls?"

Arne pinched the bridge of his nose.

"Do not annoy the Elf King of Alfheim, little man," I said, doing my best to sound giant-like.

Arne released the magic around Aaron Carlson's head. "You have a choice. Accept what we say or I kill you. It's that simple, Mr. Carlson."

Arne looked out over the lake again. "I will deal with Maura's grandfather in the morning," he said.

Carlson pointed at me. "I'm a lawyer. My firm can handle just about anything. We can help you. All of you." He shook his head. "*Elves*." Then he looked at the trees. "Those wolves. Were they..."

"Yes," I said.

Yells came from the front of the house. Arne looked Carlson up and down. He drew a pentagon of magic in the air, then slapped it onto Carlson's forehead. "If you lie, I will know."

Carlson staggered back. "I'm a *lawyer*. Listening in on my cases is going to give you a migraine."

Arne did not laugh. He pushed Carlson toward the path to the other side of the house and the fire trucks. "If Sheriff Martinez tells me you are cooperating in a manner to his liking, I will let you and your family live."

Carlson stiffened. He nodded. And together, we made our way to the other side.

CHAPTER 30

D ag, Maura, and Akeyla were already in the ambulance when I escorted Arne and Aaron Carlson to the fire trucks. Turned out that once my brother disappeared, all the elves—Arne included— began to heal at their normal, accelerated pace. Maura's face was back to smooth and lovely already, and Akeyla was sitting up, though she had a doozy of a headache.

They would spend the night at the hospital with Alfheim's elf healer, and would be home for dinner tomorrow.

Dag needed a cast. She'd done herself extra damage when she'd opened the tunnel into the fire, but would heal in a couple of weeks.

Arne sat in the back of the ambulance next to his wife. They did not touch. She barely looked at him.

I didn't ask. Arne had promised to take care of the Hawaii issue, and I suspected that Dag would hold him to his word.

Ed and Aaron Carlson were still talking when I left. I figured they would hammer out how to deal with Mrs. Carlson and the two workers who'd been thralled by my brother.

The house was a loss, but the crews managed to keep the fire from spreading into the woods. The wolves had dispersed into search teams to make sure my brother had indeed vanished.

The damage he brought with him had dissipated. The shadows lightened. My rage crawled back into the pit where I kept it. The elves sensed the change, as well. The consensus among the magical was that my brother had gone off to a hole to die for good.

The wolves would search anyway. Arne said several of the other town elves had come out and would help Gerard and Remy as needed.

Plans needed to be made and set in place, in case Brother appeared again. No one had seen the Bitersons since the library incident. I had several questions, mostly for Ivan, but Tony needed to provide a few answers as well.

Overall, we likely still had a vampire problem.

But I would leave that to the elves. Tony and Ivan had an unusual level of respect for Arne, and likely would behave, if a deal was cut.

I just wanted to go home and sleep.

I stumbled toward my cold, dark house. Only about half the string lights came on as I walked up; the fight between Arne and Brother had made a mess of my yard. Part of the fence lay in the middle of the driveway, and my artsy gate hung askew. But the house itself stood unscathed, unlike my neighbors'.

I flipped on the kitchen light before opening the French doors to my deck. The moon continued to throw a long, pale-silver slice onto the lake. At its tip, the embers and broken shards of the Carlson house glowed exactly its opposite: squat, red-gold, and above the water.

I rubbed at my face. I had a few hours before sunup. A shower first, then sleep. In the morning, I'd go into town and get myself a new phone.

Somewhere in the woods, one of the werewolves howled. I counted one, two, three... The rest of the pack joined in. They would run, search, and hunt deer. And they would come back tomorrow as the good citizens of Alfheim they had long been.

Maybe they'd find my dog.

I'd go look for him tomorrow morning, instead of sitting on the deck across from my brother's pyre. Warm my stiff, cold body with a walk in the woods. But for now, sleep beckoned.

~

I woke to a crisp, bright morning. The trees had shifted more toward the reds and golds of autumn, and rustled along the lakeshore. The Alfheim Apple Fest would be bringing more tourists to town this weekend, and likely more investors looking for cabin plots.

I donned my jeans, t-shirt, and boots, and walked out onto the deck. In the morning light, the cracks in the decking stood out, as did the elven blood stains. I'd have a day of cleaning and repair when I got home.

The trail around the lake took me into the trees and across the peninsula. No cabins on the other side yet, though a surveying crew had already marked a lot.

Birds chirped overhead. Squirrels ran the branches as if they knew I walked alone. I plodded along, hoping to catch some indication of my dog.

I whistled. "Marcus!" I yelled. "Here, boy!"

Ahead and off the trail, a dog barked.

"Marcus Aurelius!" I called.

I stepped through the brambles to make my way down to the lake.

The emperor stood on the shoreline, his head up and his tail wagging, next to a goddess.

Not a *real* goddess—if she was an actual goddess I'd have seen her magic, and though this woman had magic clinging to her, it wasn't as detailed or controlled as the elves' or any other wielders I'd met.

No, she was a human woman. A beautiful, red-haired woman in jeans and a hoodie that did not hide her perfect curves.

"Oh," I heard myself saying like an idiot. Why was I reacting this way to a random woman? Was it the soft, slight magic around her? Was it her keen eyes? She wasn't afraid of me, though she did look sad.

Marcus Aurelius obviously liked her.

"Hello," I said.

"Hello," she said, then patted Marcus's head. "Your dog came to visit me this morning."

I smiled. I couldn't help myself. She blinked and looked away, but smiled too.

Getting my hopes up would only lead to pain. No woman liked dating a walking corpse. But maybe we could be friends. "I'm Frank," I said. "Frank Victorsson."

She tucked the wallet-looking thing in her hand into the pocket of her hoodie and wiped her palms on her jeans, but then she slipped.

"Here," I said, and took her arm without thinking. Without considering how upsetting my cold fingers might be.

But she only looked up at my face with clear, thankful eyes.

She took my hand. "Thank you," she said. "I'm Ellie Jones."

She held onto my fingers. No flinching. No pulling away. Only her beautiful face saying, again, that she was not afraid of me.

Maybe all that had transpired had also expired. Maybe I'd walked out of last night's horrors and into a much better, new day.

Marcus Aurelius barked his agreement.

"Ellie Jones," I said.

The beautiful woman touching my hand went by the name Ellie Jones. She smiled again.

Yes, today would be a much better day.

And I would do everything in my power to keep it that way.

EPILOGUE

North of Alfheim, the night of the full moon....

The vampire whom the elves thought to mock with the pathetic name of "Tony Biterson" stood in the shadows of a large elm, knee-deep in underbrush, and waited for his "brother" Ivan to get their bearings. Too many trees rustled here. Too many animals hissed. The natural world did not like vampires and made a raucous noise in protest of their presence.

A coyote watched them from about twenty paces away. The animal chirped and stared, and would dash away immediately if it thought either vampire was about to make it dinner.

"You are not fast enough," Tony called. "None of you are *fast enough.*"

The animals, like the elves, had no idea who they were dealing with.

The coyote yip-howled and ran off into the trees.

Ivan tapped a hooked finger on the page of the witch's last remaining spell book. How he managed to get it out of the library before the Elf King went nuclear, Tony did not know, nor did he ask. The wielding of non-vampiric magicks was not his domain. He did, though, understand the need for outsourcing to experts, and Ivan was most definitely an expert.

Tony had done some ancestral digging before bringing Ivan into his venture. He'd checked and rechecked the little troll-man's credentials.

Witch-breed who did not implode while mortal were rare indeed, and to be of the witches *and* turned, rarer still. Ivan was a special gift Tony would not squander.

A cloth hung from Tony's back pocket—another bit of the witch's legacy Ivan had managed to save. The cloth did not like him, nor did he like it, but it did not have the power to compel him to abandon it.

So he'd carried it into the woods when he and Ivan had run from Arne Odinsson. Running was not Tony's best moment, but the running had a purpose, and was part of the greater plan.

A plan that utilized Tony's best traits.

He was stealth and disguise. Spying and intrigue. Using an enemy's most easily-manipulated traits against them. With the elves of Alfheim, that trait was their incessant need to be "modern."

Everyone could be rehabilitated, in the modern world. The mundanes had built entire economies around rehabilitating the different, the naughty, and the straight-up bad.

Part of Arne Odinsson's rehabilitation was to become a kinder, gentler ruler. A man who no longer slaughtered to take territory, but instead built the shining town on the hill and invited in the unloved. "*Look!* We have nice doggies and nice biters here in Alfheim! I'm the best Elf King on Earth. The best. So wonderful and incredible, I've been keeping a walking corpse as a pet for two full centuries."

Tony had known the moment he first met Frank Victorsson that he was looking at the mundane version of the rumors. "There is one of us," the rumors whispered. "One Who is Many. Many Who are One."

No vampire attended to the rumors; they were whispers and not prophecy. But Tony listened. Tony had reasons. Tony wanted to know what "One Who is Many" meant, and who those "many" might be.

Frank Victorsson's walking patchwork corpse gave the rumors

validity, and in Tony's mind, a hint of prophecy. What else could Mr. Victorsson be other than a marker of something greater? He was a first draft and first drafts were often revised.

So Tony and Ivan stopped among the elves and the sparkly white magic. Tony charmed. Ivan found a source of darkness to feed his needs. They dipped and they bowed and they waited.

Their first attempt, in the sixties, put blood in the water. Their second attempt, in the eighties, almost exploded in their faces. For a while, they'd wondered if the vampire that drove Ed Martinez north was the vampire they sought, but no. He'd been the wrong kind of crazy and had gotten himself staked by the mundane.

Then that pathetic, lovesick fire spirit poked holes in Alfheim's defenses from the *outside*, and they knew they could send out the correct call for the correct vampire.

The true ruler. The One. The Only.

Tony rubbed his hands together. The birch blocked most of the moonlight, but he was one of the lovelies, the vampires who thralled through beauty, and he carried an unearthly shimmer that mundanes sensed but did not see. It made him stand out in a crowd, but under the moon, it became visible.

He'd learned to control its brilliance a long time ago. Age did have its benefits, and for vampires, it usually meant increased control of their demon blood and its many side effects.

Ivan had a similar sheen, but his had more to do with his manipulation of magicks than the moon.

Ivan was not a lovely. Ivan was Ivan, and even Tony knew better than to ask about how he'd turned.

"Well?" Tony asked. He could, though, ask about the meddling they did.

Ivan held up his hand. He closed his squinty eyes and pointed with his crooked finger. "Ash?" he hissed.

Tony sniffed in the direction of Ivan's pointing. "Yes." He clasped Ivan's shoulder. "You are worthy of the coming New Order, my friend."

Ivan chittered in much the same way as the coyote had.

Tony knocked through the underbrush. "Come," he said.

They pushed through the thickets and the leaves, both with their heads low and their vampire senses queued toward their goal: The One Who is Many.

Tony pressed between the trunks of two large trees and stepped into a small hole in the forest. Dead birches and brambles framed the space. The limb of a dead oak formed a roof that shaded from both moon and sun. The ground, devoid of plant life, writhed with beetles and worms.

This was a place of dying. Not a place of death—too much lived around it, and in its floor. Decay wafted from the soil and rotting leaves. It was a place of transition from The Land of the Living to The Land of the Dead.

Most forests had such spots. They were few and far between, and protected by a primordial magic that made them undetectable to elves, fae, and wolves, though Tony had heard that the kami could find such locations if they set their minds to it.

Tony gingerly set his foot down onto the mass of bugs and peered into the black shadows. "Many Who is One?" he called.

Something skittered. Something else slithered. An inhale followed, then chewing noises.

Tony had his phone. He could turn on the light. But light meant that he feared—and fear, now, would only get him killed.

He glanced over his shoulder. "Ivan," he said. "Hold up your book."

His small friend shuffled. Paper rustled. "See," he hissed, and spread wide the pages.

The shadows did not part. Light did not enter, yet borders formed between different blacknesses, and angles took on clarity. Centipedes left spotted trails and beetles dotted lines. Grain popped up out of old wood. And He Whom They Sought crouched in the center, half a rabbit in his hand and his face covered with blood.

In his shoulder, the remains of Hel's Dagger continued to smoke. Tony stepped closer and peered at the wound.

The giant vampire growled.

Tony raised his hand. "There, there," he said, and pointed at the wound. "You have a piece of Odin's gallows in your shoulder," he said.

The giant snorted and went back to gnawing on his rabbit.

Slowly, carefully, Tony wrapped the witch's linen around his hand. "Allow me to check your wound."

He reached for the bit of the Dagger still poking through the giant's skin. And just as slowly and carefully, he twisted.

The linen smoked. It did not like the Dagger and heat roared up Tony's hand, but he continued to hold on.

The giant dropped the rabbit. He gagged and rubbed at his eyes. "Where am I?" he said in a clear, unambiguous Scottish accent.

"No, no," Ivan hissed from the brambles. "Not The One?"

Tony shot his hand toward the Dagger and twisted it once again. More heat, but he pulled back the cloth quickly enough that it did not catch fire.

Under the weave of the linen, Tony's skin blistered. He reveled in the pain, in the tactile sense of it, but he would need to be fast. If he lost the cloth, he would no longer be able to adjust the Dagger's alignment with the universe. And without adjustment, one of the Many who was not The One might retain control.

Or the combined personality might re-emerge. And Tony doubted he and Ivan could keep the combined Many under control.

Better to find The One.

The giant rambled something in an old East Asian language, one that Tony did not recognize. Behind him, Ivan chattered again.

The next twist dialed up a Frenchman. The next a Caribbean slave who, when The One Who Is Many was constructed, must have been as feral as the part who had been eating the rabbit. The slave, though, rattled off a rant about hoodoo and Caribbean gods.

The cloth smoked as much as the Dagger, and the burn climbed Tony's arm. His skin puckered and his nerves screamed.

He hadn't felt this real since he was alive. He hooted and twisted the blade again.

The cloth ignited. Tony yelled and dropped it to the scurrying beetles underfoot. Whoever of the Many he'd dialed up would be the One with whom they would walk forward.

The giant inhaled. He pulled back from Tony's touch. He roared at the dead oak roof over their heads. Then he stood tall and laughed.

He wiped the remains of the rabbit from his person before holding up his hands and examining his new body. "Well, well," he said. "Fascinating."

Tony knew the voice issuing from the giant. He understood intimately the new set to the creature's shoulders, and the straightness of his back.

They had found The True One.

"You were stitched together," Tony said. "Built from the parts of many of your children."

The giant laughed. "How very... cyclical." He examined his hands again. "And ironic."

"The modern mundanes would call your state 'meta,'" Tony said.

The One chortled. "Mundanes and their ridiculous hackneyed murder of language."

As vampires, they did understand murder, hackneyed or otherwise.

The One stretched his massive neck. "It was like a dream, being among the vampire dead." He snapped his fingers. "Waiting."

Tony also stood, and Tony also wiped remains from his person, though his were of beetles and bugs. "I did my best to facilitate your speedy recovery." He nodded toward the brambles. "There is another with a body like this one. He, too, is a sum of his parts. He allowed your return."

The giant nodded before placing his hand over the Dagger. Like Tony, he could not touch the wood. He *humphed* and the entrance point vanished under a layer of ash.

"We do not truly die a second time," Tony said. "I knew you would await my call."

The giant laughed again, then gripped Tony's shoulder in much the same way Tony had gripped Ivan's earlier.

Tony would not wince under his brother's painful grip. "I *knew,* when I heard the rumors," he said. "I asked myself, 'Who would an idiot scientist dig up and use as a base for his best work?'"

The giant formed and reformed the ash around his body, first as a nice business suit, then as a Victorian gentleman's outfit, then as the armor Tony remembered from his days riding under his brother's command against the Ottoman Empire.

"I no longer have mine," Tony said, as he pointed at the ash-formed Dracul crest over the giant's semi-beating heart.

"I do believe my true armor would no longer fit." The giant laughed again. "This… construction… is fascinating." He stretched out his arms and the armor contracted, once again, to a business suit.

This time, the giant clasped both of Tony's shoulders. "Thank you, little brother," he said. "Thank you for believing in the sanctity of our family."

Tony would no longer allow the elves of Alfheim to call him Tony Biterson, nor would he feign thankfulness for their benevolence. No, he now had what he needed to build a true vampire empire—and to finish the task he and his brother had started long ago.

The vampire no longer called Tony had pulled from The Many the True One, the master vampire, the man whose willpower had given the demons of The Land of the Dead a purpose.

He had returned Vlad the Impaler to The Land of the Living.

Radu the Handsome held his head high. "You are welcome, my brother."

Vlad laughed once again. "Come, Radu," he said. "Introduce me to your friend. Ivan, is it?" He walked toward the passage between the trees.

In the moonlight, Ivan blinked and bowed, and Vlad clasped his hands behind his back. "Such a lovely world," he said, then he stretched to his full height. "Shall we make it ours?"

Word of mouth and reviews are vital to the success of any author. If

you enjoyed **Monster Born** please consider leaving a review. Even
one sentence would be useful for other readers.
Thank you!

JOIN FRANK VICTORSSON and the rest of Alfheim in **Vampire
Cursed**....

VAMPIRE CURSED

CHAPTER 1

She told me her name was Ellie Jones and that I wouldn't remember her in the morning. She smiled a small, sad smile when she said it, one of those knowing smiles that made me believe she had lost hope. Ellie Jones believed that no matter what happened, come morning, she would be an afterthought.

Magic wafted around her like thin wisps of blue, purple, and green smoke. Not strong, obviously organized magic, but where she walked, subtle sheets of Aurora Borealis energy trailed.

The same magic that moved her to this place. Magic hurt her friend and it hurt her. It picked her up and it thrashed her against the rocks of my shore.

The magic meant she spoke the truth. Only magic could enchant and conceal—and wipe memories. Only magic could weigh on someone's shoulders the way it weighed on hers.

"I will remember you," I said. There were ways around enchantments.

I came to this side of my lake—through the woods of the peninsula to the span of water out of view of my home—looking for my lost dog.

I found him, and he'd found Ellie....

Order **Vampire Cursed** today.

THE WORLDS OF

KRIS AUSTEN RADCLIFFE

Smart Urban Fantasy:

Northern Creatures
Monster Born
Vampire Cursed
Elf Raised
Wolf Hunted
Fae Touched
Death Kissed (*coming soon*)

*Genre-bending Science Fiction about
love, family, and dragons:*

WORLD ON FIRE
Series one
Fate Fire Shifter Dragon
Games of Fate

Flux of Skin
Fifth of Blood
Bonds Broken & Silent
All But Human
Men and Beasts
The Burning World

Dragon's Fate and Other Stories

Series Two
Witch of the Midnight Blade
Witch of the Midnight Blade Part One
Witch of the Midnight Blade Part Two
Witch of the Midnight Blade Part Three

Witch of the Midnight Blade: The Complete Series

Series Three
World on Fire
Call of the Dragonslayer (*coming soon*)

Hot Contemporary Romance:

The Quidell Brothers
Thomas's Muse
Daniel's Fire
Robert's Soul
Thomas's Need
Andrew's Kiss (*coming soon*)

Quidell Brothers Box Set
Includes:

Thomas's Muse
Daniel's Fire
Roberts's Soul

ABOUT THE AUTHOR

Kris's Science Fiction universe, **World on Fire**, brings her descriptive touch to the fantastic. Her Urban Fantasy series, **Northern Creatures**, sets her magic free. She's traversed many storytelling worlds including dabbles in film and comic books, spent time as a talent agent and a textbook photo coordinator, as well written nonfiction. But she craved narrative and richly-textured worlds—and unexpected, true love.

Kris lives in Minnesota with one husband, two daughters, and three cats.

For more information
www.krisaustenradcliffe.com

Made in the USA
Las Vegas, NV
11 November 2020

10703925R00125